About the Author

Bernard Ashley is one of the most highly regarded authors in this country. Born in Woolwich, south London, he was evacuated during the war, and ended up attending fourteen different primary schools. After school, Bernard did National Service in the RAF where he 'flew' a typewriter. He then went on to become a teacher and later a headteacher – his two most recent posts being in east and south London, areas which have provided him with the settings for many of his books. Bernard now writes full time.

Bernard Ashley's other novels for the Black Apple list include *Tiger Without Teeth*, a *Guardian* Book of the Week, and *Little Soldier*, which was shortlisted for the *Guardian* Children's Book Award and the Carnegie Medal.

'Bernard Ashley's greatest gift is to turn what seems to be low-key realism into something much stronger and more resonant.' *Philip Pullman*

D0529222

ALSO BY BERNARD ASHLEY

LITTLE SOLDIER

*Shortlisted for the Carnegie Medal and
the Guardian Children's Book Award*

TIGER WITHOUT TEETH

*The extract from Rudyard Kipling's 'A Smuggler's Song' from
'Puck of Pook's Hill', 1906, is reproduced by kind permission of
AP Watt Ltd, on behalf of The National Trust for Places
of Historical Interest or Natural Beauty.*

ORCHARD BOOKS
96 Leonard Street
London EC2A 4XD
Orchard Books Australia
Unit 31/56 O'Riordan Street, Alexandria, NSW 2015
1 84121 814 6
A paperback original
First published in Great Britain in 2002
Text © Bernard Ashley 2002
The right of Bernard Ashley to be identified as the author of this
work has been asserted by him in accordance with the Copyright,
Designs and Patents Act, 1988.
A CIP catalogue record for this book is
available from the British Library.
1 3 5 7 9 10 8 6 4 2
Printed in Great Britain

REVENGE HOUSE

Bernard Ashley

ORCHARD BOOKS

I should like to thank Iris Ashley,
Ed and Gloria Holbrook, Edgar Francis and
Terry Mott for their help with
my research for this book.

CHAPTER ONE

'What d'you reckon? Good or not good?'

'Good. Brilliant!' Sophia Micheli said.

Her best friend Elise had been coming to Club Seventeen a couple of weeks longer and looked delighted at the Micheli smile.

'And he's a nice bloke, that one,' Eli said.

'Jon?' Sophia shrugged. 'Yeah, he was OK...'

Eli clung on to the bus handrail as it took the High Road like a runaway stagecoach. '*Jon?* You mean *Jonny*.' She pulled an embarrassed face on Sophia's behalf. 'No one ever calls him *Jon*.'

'I did!' Sophia clung too. 'He never said anything: I reckoned that was his name. Jon Elite. Like, *Jon Special*, a cut above, I even told him...'

Eli screeched laughing, now in Sophia's face, now away in the bounce of the bus. 'Sofe, you bonzo! It's Jonny Leete. Off the Paxton estate. *Jon Elite* – yeah, I'll just bet he liked that, the toff!' But Eli was a mate. 'Next week just call him Jonny. Make nothing of it.

And ask him if he's got a friend for me!'

The bus jerked to a halt, the usual sticking brakes. Sophia jumped out of the double doors, more pushed than sprung. She waved to Eli who was going on another couple of stops and dived into Boots' doorway to take a wet wipe to her mouth: then her eyes: she'd gone out without make-up, she'd better go in without it – who wanted World War Three?

'*You've got make-up on!*'

'*So has Eddie Izzard.*'

'*He's a transvestite.*'

'*Can I wear Dad's suit?*'

A typical exchange between her and her mother: Sophia Micheli of the New Girls and Lesley Micheli, a theatre designer who was always more used to stress than calm. She and Sophia were two cats you wouldn't put in one sack, so it had been a giant stride for womankind, Sophia getting a night out until ten. With her dad working evenings her mother had been as happy as headaches about letting her out with Eli: but her dad had satisfied himself that the Italian Association's Under-Eighteen Saturday disco was clean of drugs, given her a lecture on handling herself – and she'd gone. There was no need to abort all future missions before she got back through the door on this one.

Sophia checked in the little mirror she kept with

her make-up under the cardboard bottom of her shoulder bag. All clear. Except her mother could see glitter in a sunburst, white confetti in a snowstorm. No matter how thick the canvas side of a homework hold-all she'd always see right on through the text books to the *Teenscene* magazine. Which Sophia bought on purpose to get her going.

'*You wasting your money again?*'

'*Like water through my fingers!*'

Tonight her mother would have been reading the time like a book she couldn't put down, waiting for her to be safe indoors from the dangers of north London at night. Her dad had swung this – girls had to be shown a bit of trust at her age – so a big row when she got in would have held no chance of a victory; not over going out on Saturdays to Club Seventeen. If she wanted him to get good reports, Sophia had to work for them.

She pulled the black sweater out of her bag and slipped it on, making a face as she buttoned her blouse two holes higher. She loosened her belt and lowered her skirt. Still not enough, she started walking with a slight bend to her knees so her legs didn't look so long and bare, and she tried to fill her mind with worthy thoughts of nice little school friends and RE homework, anything to take the fizz from the Bullseye she'd drunk and push out Jonny

Leete who'd sweet-talked her about Spurs. And with an impersonation of being in the right frame of mind, she hit the button of the bell.

Her mother didn't come straight off, no doubt playing it cool: no whipping open the door and asking, 'Where have you been?' Instead she took her time. Then, 'Where have you been?'

'If you think this is late…'

'I didn't say that.' All the same, there was a look at her watch and a wobble of her head.

'And Eli and I had a really good time, thanks.'

'Fine.'

Sophia headed for the stairs. She needed a bright light to check for sure on the make-up.

'There's removing pads in the cabinet.'

'Excellent.'

Sophia didn't change her tight expression – but, *Mamma-Mia*, she'd got the enemy on the run! It was like being bought her first bra – when she'd wanted black and got it; threatening to let things hang free otherwise.

And that was that. Sophia Micheli went clubbing at the Seventeen on Saturday nights.

On that Saturday night, three miles south-west, Piccadilly Circus was all clubbers. And tourists and punters and pushers. Further along the street in

Leicester Square, portraits would still be drawn at midnight and roses would be bought for women betrayed. Traffic clogged, people milled, dips took wallets, bars spilled out and queues lined up at the club doors; mostly girls in off the shoulder tattooes and skimpy skirts, swinging handbags fatter than their bellies. It was all as bright as day, just differently coloured, with neon adverts on the move and the flashing of police emergency blue, everything rowdier than a riot with the talk and shout and scream, the rev of cars and the whoop of sirens. London never really sleeps, it just works at getting unconscious.

Through this lot weaved Sophia's father, Antonio Micheli, his saxophone in its plush case, his eighth stint that week in the theatre orchestra for *Carousel* all done and Sunday off tomorrow. Right now he had to cross Regent Street and get to Piccadilly Circus tube – the Bakerloo line to Oxford Circus and the Victoria line out to Seven Sisters – a journey that would take him forty minutes at the outside; with Sophia, please Holy Mary, safe indoors from her big night out at Club Seventeen. He'd thought of her a lot during the performance tonight, his fingers crossed for her safety: and he'd nearly missed a sax entrance in the second act, worrying about her, so he couldn't wait to get home through the West End crush.

He stood by the crossing lights at the front of a

swelling crowd. A surge of girls who'd not got into the Galaxy club were heading towards Shaftesbury Avenue to Xtreme – all Wrigley's gum, Mayfair fags and shivering shoulders. He looked at them and knew Lesley would have made Sophia take a top coat or a sweater, not let her walk the Seven Sisters Road half naked like these; back home in his Alássio she would have worn more in the sun than these girls wore in the cold. But that was life. You lived twenty-first century in the city or you didn't live at all. Life was all about where the work was, what was around you, you took it on at its own strength.

And right now what was around Sophia's father was frustration; kids worried they were missing out on a Saturday night's clubbing. The crossing lights still gave them the little red man but they were jostling for the green like a pack of distance runners.

'It's up there.'

'Round the left.'

'I know a guy on the door...'

Snorts.

'I did! Once.'

'He let you in?'

'Nah.'

'Useful!'

And the red man went, the green man came. Like a swollen river breaching a dam the girls rushed into the road, a surge of shoulders and straps – and with the flow, unable to stop himself, Antonio Micheli was swept forward. Helpless, he saw a dirty white van heading straight for him from the left, a revving Transit chased by the flashing blue and the screaming siren of a police car. The van was shooting across the lights and squealing towards Haymarket – and there was no stopping its foot-down driver who wanted away and who had the road. Except that Sophia's father was in the way, pushed into the van's path in the rush to cross. It was fifty-fifty as to who the winner would be – and fifty-fifty always goes the driver's way.

The van's offside hit Antonio Micheli hard on the left of his pelvis. It threw him up and to the side where his head hit with a sick thud on the sharp metal of street furniture – the upright of a sign showing the way ahead: the van not stopping, nor the girls, who were screaming at the near miss, but still running for entry into Xtreme.

'Wa's 'is name?'

'On the door? Didn't say. Who does, up West?'

And those were the last words Antonio Micheli ever heard, his body as battered as his mangled saxophone in its case.

He would have been no more than a dead maggot in a seething wound to the man looking down from the first floor office of Galaxy Club. Downstairs the place was two-step thumping, but up here it was quieter – in more ways than one. Crucial to this man, there was no noise on the phone line, it wasn't being tapped by the police. The Galaxy wasn't his club in the sense that he didn't own it, but then it was his, in the sense that he had the seamy side of the West End all sewn up. If Frank Leonard wanted to come calling, he came calling; and tonight he wanted to come calling. His manor house down in Kent was bugged, without doubt; he couldn't trust an electricity socket, and the phones had the faintest echo to them as if they were plugged into deep space. Mobiles, too. He might as well have held all his conversations on the fifth floor of Scotland Yard. But Dave Sewell's Galaxy Club was still clean, it hadn't been open long enough for the law to get tapping, so for an expected phone call which needed to be secret this was a good place to be.

Frank Leonard was a small man who looked like Hitler without the moustache: he had the same lizard eyes and his mouth was always puckered tight as if he were digesting something bad. People watched out for themselves if ever he smiled. Not that the locals saw much of him at all behind the high walls of Middle Marsh Manor in the quiet Kent countryside, a real contrast to the London – the noisy, sweaty, crowded capital – where he liked to be. London was where he operated: protection, earnings from girls, gambling, and biggest of all, drugs. And where he'd killed. He'd already done life for a punishment murder, he knew where the remains of other East Enders could be found if the fishes hadn't eaten them; and he wouldn't think twice about breaking an arm or scalding a pretty city girl. No one in the capital ever said no to Frank Leonard if he wanted a favour. The man had power, and it paid to fear him.

The phone rang in the office. He turned away from the window and nodded to Sewell to answer it.

'Galaxy.'

The voice at the other end must have said something meaningful. Without a word the club owner gave the phone to Leonard and left the room fast: no one wanted to know anything they didn't need to know about this man's activities.

'Yeah?' Leonard said. He listened. 'You're saying it's gone through, it's *on*, it's a "go", right?' He listened some more, and without another word put down the phone and left the office – heading for the underground car park and the A20 to Kent. And on his face was the beginning of a smile.

By two a.m. Lesley Micheli was getting worried. Sophia could tell. Upstairs, she couldn't sleep, with the sound of Saturday night sirens up and down the Seven Sisters Road, and so much to go over in her head. Downstairs, her mother would know the same as she did – that the show always finished to the minute and the band was always out before the exit doors opened. Her dad was never late. She could hear her mother at the kettle, then at it again a half hour later; then at the front door, then making another cup of tea.

Which was when the police came. First the murmur of voices, someone being kind, followed by her mother suddenly screaming as Sophia ran for the stairs. She burst into the room to see Lesley whimpering and shivering, a policewoman's arm round her shoulder. She rushed to her mother, stared into her face asking the question to which she already knew the answer. Her father was dead.

'How? *Why?*'

Sophia felt her mother's questions through their chest bones, two cats now without claws. The policewoman muttered something about a drug-dealing suspect jumping the lights.

Lesley wiped a hand across her eyes. 'Toni. Where is he?'

'Middlesex Hospital.'

'And there's no chance...?'

The policeman shook his head. 'No, love. No chance.'

And Lesley Micheli wailed like the bereaved of all the world. 'He wasn't the one I was worried about not coming back!' She hugged Sophia hard, shaking, hurting – hugging, but somehow as if Sophia had changed the pattern by going out; Sophia had made tonight different. And Sophia held her in return, standing tall, her legs as long as she liked; not crying herself because she couldn't – right now she was having to be the strength.

'This sick bloody place!' Lesley's wretched face wailed at the whole of London. Sophia held on to her as she swayed, and led her towards a chair, where she collapsed and cringed and shook.

The policeman crackled something into his radio, all in code for the sake of the bereaved. He went to find the kettle, which hadn't cooled all evening. Sophia slid round to where she could hold her mother's hand, itself as cold as death. She murmured meaningless words into her ear, but they were across a divide – there was nothing she could think to say in comfort for either of them. Her dad hadn't been ill, he'd been on top musical form, he wasn't old, he didn't have troubles, and he'd loved, loved, loved her. And he was gone. For ever.

The need nagged at her till she was alone – and that was nearly dawn, having hugged and cried her mother to sleep. Sophia took out the brass-locked diary her father had given her on her birthday and opened it for the first time, something almost too hard to do with her shaking fingers and its little key, and inside it she started to write what she couldn't live without beginning tonight, the words of a daughter's song for him:

You used to walk tall through that door,
To tell me what was right from wrong,
Smile with stories from the show,
Blow a sax from the room below.
And now that sinner's killed your song—
Silenced you for ever more.
But I will always sing to you
In private scribbles, solos sung—
Of who I am and where I go:
Verses for Antonio.

'This bastard London!' Lesley suddenly woke and shouted. 'Crooks, noise, smell, traffic, *death*!' Her voice croaked and she whimpered in her bed like a three-year-old who'd lost her mother in the market. 'My Toni!' And again she wailed the house down.

Frank Leonard's white Mercedes slid through the gates of Middle Marsh Manor. It crunched round the driveway and didn't slow for the cat in its path. The cat moved or it died: braking too hard made ruts in the gravel. The cat jumped and the car drove on into the stable-block garage, the door automatic.

Getting out, Frank Leonard went through into the dark house. He skirted the indoor pool and came to the kitchen where he found a tin of tonic in the fridge. His ears cocked to the sound of a shuffle at the door, but he didn't turn. His wife Bev stood in the doorway, tall, long legged, still holding herself well. She was twenty years younger than him, once a svelte blonde model, travelling to Parkhurst every visiting time permitted. She'd been asleep upstairs; sheet lines ran down her belly.

'You want some supper or anything, Frankie?' She put a hand behind her head, didn't move otherwise.

'No – I got some thinking to do.'

'Thought you might want something...'

He swore at her. 'I told you, I got some thinking to do.' He turned the tap on full, switched on the radio. 'Someone I want is on the move.'

A lift of her chin asked who.

'Someone transferring prisons, Wyck Hill to Garside.'

'Got a name, has he?'

'That's nothing to you.'

Bev pouted. 'You used to tell me these things, Frankie. We used to share all sorts...'

'Well we don't now.'

'I used to be your friend...' Bev stopped herself and turned away. 'Then you have got some thinking to do,' she said. 'All on your own.' And she went back to bed, pretending not to hear the curt filthy name he called her.

From your loving wife. Rest peaceful, my darling Toni. Les. XXX

Lesley's flower arrangement was small, blue and purple, and discreet. Sophia's was a single white carnation, her dad's traditional buttonhole on opening nights.

To the best Dad, the coolest sax in the world – from your girl Sophia. XXXXX

Antonio Micheli's widowed mother – Sophia's *nonna* – fat and slow and devastated in black – had had her son's name posted in black-edged bills on the streets of Alássio. All today in north London she was being helped in and out of cars, on and off seats by an uncle who'd come with her; while Sophia's other grandparents had come from Leeds and were bustling and busy with the practical things. What Sophia wanted was a cuddle from someone, but all she got was wailing on one side and cups of tea on the other.

The ceremony was Catholic and long, the responses drowned in the drone of A10 lorries; and the burial in the Roman Catholic grounds of Enfield Cemetery was lost in the noise of urban life under a Heathrow flight path where the heavy jets thundered in on final approaches; all so loud that Sophia had to strain to hear the earth hit her father's coffin. But the louder sound that she knew she'd hear for ever was the brass section from her dad's show standing at the graveside, playing 'You'll Never Walk Alone'. She clutched at Eli's hand and shook, the way she'd shaken on their rattling bus home the night he died.

'Take me away!' Lesley gritted to her brother Mike, the widow suddenly pulling from the gaping hole. People made way, and Sophia went too.

'Where?' asked Mike. 'In the vestry? You want to go to the car?' He was supporting her like the walking wounded.

Lesley straightened like a stick and turned to face him with wild eyes. 'No! Get me away from all this!' She shook her black-gloved fist at a 747 going over low. 'I want to be where there's peace and quiet! Away from crooks and racket and London filth!' And with her hands clamped over both her ears she ran like someone shell shocked towards the busy road.

CHAPTER TWO

Sophia had just walked in from school.

'I want a word with you.'

'I'm here, aren't I?'

'What the hell do you think you're playing at?'

'I beg your pardon!'

The start of the first row. But it was Sophia who was pointing the finger and it was Lesley on the back foot. A month after the death of their man and they were at one another's throats, Lesley still in black, Sophia in her school uniform. She'd just said 'See you!' to Eli and come through the door to find her mother on the telephone to a house agent, serious – talking very serious – about selling up.

'*You* were upset at the cemetery – Mary, Mother of God, wasn't *I* upset?!' Sophia went on.

'Don't blaspheme, please.'

'Who cares? I bet God cares more about what you're doing to me right now!'

'Which is nothing wrong!' Lesley was working up to anger now.

'Madre, you had every right to be upset at the funeral…'

'Thank you!'

'Like the rest of us. We were all upset. Nonna was. I was. *I was!* I *am* his daughter, or was, or have you forgotten?' Sophia threw her school bag across the sitting room into a corner, rocking a tall floor lamp. She ruffled her cropped hair, hard. 'We know how he died and we all hate that scum. We all hated that bloody cemetery with all the aeroplanes and the noise—'

'*But?*'

'But that's no reason now to chase us off out of where we live. Where *I* live, where Eli and my friends are, where my education is…'

'Oh, you're worried about your education? That's news!'

Sophia's skin had gone cold and her stomach had hardened. She wanted to swipe at her mother for that quick, cocky reply – better to slam out of the room before she went too far. But she stayed. Typical.

'I'm worried about my *life*!' she shouted. 'I live here, this is where I belong…' Sophia waved her arms around the room, took in Tottenham and the whole of north London. 'This is *me*! This is Sophia Micheli!'

Lesley thumped her own chest. 'And this is *me*! And you belong where your mother decides! Christ, girl—'

'Don't blaspheme, please!'

'—people move about! Your father moved about! We all – move about!'

'For a reason. For jobs, for getting married…'

Lesley suddenly slowed it. 'And for getting widowed, Sophia! I want out of crooked, hateful London!' – she waved some sheets of properties into Sophia's face – 'and, what's more, we're going!'

Sophia just stared at her angry, distraught mother, couldn't think of anything more to say that wouldn't be over the top hysterical.

'Listen,' Lesley came down from boiling point to a simmer, 'all of this here is him and me.' Now she waved her arms around the room. 'Everything's a memory, even what I do, what I did, my theatre work. That's all about that life, the old Lesley Micheli. I want a new start away from everything this place and London say to me…'

Sophia threw herself backwards into an armchair. 'That's stupid!' she said. 'This place and London say you're just starting to make a name for yourself. So where are you dragging me to? Somewhere I can keep in touch with Eli?'

Lesley stood looking at her, pursed her lips,

unpursed them, ignored the compliment. 'I'm *dragging* you where I want!' she said – as she went to the phone to grab up her estate agents' notes.

It was all sky. Where north London was tall office walls and high-rise flats, Romney Marsh was low grass and clear air from the ankles up to heaven. Sophia stood on the empty road in front of the house and looked out across the flatness towards the sea. Half an hour earlier her mother had stood here and opened wide her arms and lifted her face up to the sun, turning her head from side to side in a slow appreciation of this space and its peace. How sad could you get? Standing in the same place now, Sophia shivered. It was so quiet you could hear a newt breathing. Spooky! To her and Eli, quiet was an intrusion into your thoughts; down here she'd know a squeaky bike was coming from half a mile away. Nearby, a bird twittered and a sheep on the marshland baa'ed. Otherwise, nothing. So much of boring *nothing*.

Sophia had been all over the remote, long-empty House – For Sale behind her, now she was out of the way while her mother and Uncle Mike talked inside to the estate agent. She didn't want another row, not here, they'd have been heard over the Channel in France. If she'd been inside the house she'd have had to shout her mother's stupidity at her again, wanting to pack up and run away from London to the country. Her dear dad wasn't cold in his grave and she was taking them away from everything he'd known and stood for. Antonio Micheli was from Italy, he was cosmopolitan, he'd played clarinet and sax at the opera in Rome and come to live the London life after he'd met Lesley on a show she'd helped design. City show biz was what he'd been about; and her, too. As Lesley Bates she'd been a Leeds, then a London, girl; as Lesley Micheli she'd been a designer on shows that toured the biggest cities in the world. Now she was after crawling under the country blankets and hiding herself down on the marshes. Just for herself. As for Sophia, well, what Club Seventeen girl who knew Jon Elite wanted to live her life where a sheep having a baa was big news?

'Got two names, this place.'

Sophia jumped. It was so quiet and *nothing* here that she hadn't heard someone come from nowhere. But he had – an old man standing on the grass verge, stooped, smiling, with the sort of face you saw on the trunks of old trees in Finsbury Park, wearing a flat cap which looked even older than he did. A sudden thought came out of nowhere – marsh spirit. Was he a will o' the wisp? But there weren't such things – he was probably just a dirty old man; you got them all over. He took off his cap to wipe it down his face. 'Marsh End, that's what you see there.' His voice was high, and rustled like tissue.

So? Sophia looked. The house sign nailed to the tree certainly said Marsh End. He could read, this yokel.

'That's new, though, that is.'

She didn't move a face muscle. With Eli she'd have put a finger under one eye and pulled the skin down. Who are you trying to kid, sunshine? *New?* The house sign was rotting.

'Belonged to a stranger, not a man o' the marsh. Never took a fancy to what it was called, so he changed the name.'

We were on to local history now! Some bonzo country gaffer living in the past.

'You look round here.' The old man walked to the side of the long house.

For a flash Sophia wondered if he'd disappear if she blinked, go as suddenly as he'd come. Please! But he seemed harmless enough and she followed on after him – well, if he disappeared, perhaps she would, too: and that'd be a result! Pop up in the Tottenham High Road.

'Judge the frame o' that door.' He twisted his body over and squinted at the building as if he could get any shorter than he was, looking at it.

'Low, ain't it, no regular size?'

Sophia looked at the side door. It was certainly small, and at an angle. The rest of the house had tall windows and a wide front door. Inside, the rooms were high ceilinged downstairs, a bit smaller up – but nothing she'd seen was as squat as this old slanting door.

'Ships' timbers they used, this end of the house. The original house.'

'Did they?' She could be polite, when she wanted.

'Old men o' war, hearts of oak. Built their houses wi' any broken up bits of ship they could get their hands on.'

'Re-cycled.'

'*Re-venge*.' He was looking at her hard and very knowing.

'Revenge?'

'*Revenge*, that was her name. Man o' war with Nelson. These timbers have seen some blood an' guts, I'll tell you... Trafalgar – did for the Frenchies' *Aigle* when things was getting hot, and then she beaches up over at Sheerness.'

'We all beach up somewhere,' Sophia said, looking round at the nothingness.

'Been empty a good spell, needs a breath o' Romney air inside it. Your mum and dad looking to buy it?' He was walking to the front again, staring at the grey stone building as if he were pricing it up.

Sophia didn't know what business it was of his, but she put him straight.

'It's not my dad, it's my uncle.'

'Aye. A lot tell you that.' But he didn't say it in a nasty way, just matter of fact. 'Fred Kiff, that's me. An' tell 'em I can turn me hand to anything. So if your uncle gets stuck, or don't know a pantile from a pancake, I'm only down the road.'

Sophia looked down the road. Only? *Country* only! There wasn't a dwelling between where she stood and the sea.

'Only three mile, along the coast a yard or two. But on the tel-e-phone.' He spelled it out the way people pronounce the name of a new ice-cream.

'I'll tell 'em.'

'An' say if they want the old sign I've got it, in me yard. Revenge House. Rightly belongs here.'

'Rightly does.'

And he was gone. But Sophia saw how he went. Running alongside the road was a dyke, the water about two metres down a bank. Tied below was a small boat, which Fred Kiff wriggled away as fast as a marsh eel. So that was how he'd come from nowhere. Everything has an explanation: like coming out at Paxton Road by knowing the short cuts of N17. There's always a trick to living, wherever you are.

*

Fishing was a tasty way of being alone. No one was putting microphones in seagulls yet, so out on the Rye fishing boat where the wind sucked words out of the mouth Frank Leonard could talk as loudly as he liked. And this Sunday morning his seasick guest was a man more used to making waves than riding them. He was Bri Tingle from Bethnal Green: the big man who emptied pubs just by walking into them, who ran a 'door firm' of club bouncers, the out-and-out muscle mostly worked by Frank Leonard's brain. Tingle had heaved more than one assassination off the side of the *Pleasant Surprise*. But he never got over the seasickness.

'This gonna take long, Frank?' Tingle asked. 'Only I ain't got no more breakfast to bring up.'

'Not all that. But you can't come out in a boat and go straight back. Everyone's on a smuggling run to these coastguards, suspicious gits. If we go back in before we've got a catch they'll take my planks apart looking for what else I've netted.'

So they fished while the boat's skipper kept the business side of the *Pleasant Surprise* away from shore binoculars. Tingle went through the motions but Leonard was skilful and savage, throwing nothing back, however small. And they talked as they gutted and threw offal at seagulls.

'There's a "shanghai" on, Bri. They're moving Donoghue...'

'Frenchie? That scum!'

'Wyck Hill to Garside, seven, eight weeks' time.'

'Yeah? Who told you, someone on the inside?'

Leonard eyed up a seagull. 'Never you mind. But I'm gonna know where, an' what route; I'm gonna get the whisper just as it's gonna be.' Leonard ripped into a fish as if it were an enemy. 'What I want from you—'

'You've 'ad me breakfast, Frank, an' me dinner – an' I've not eaten that yet...'

'So what I want now is your guts. You didn't think this was for pleasure, did you?' Leonard very nearly smiled – he loved discomfort.

'No, mate, I didn't.' Tingle was the only man on any patch who could say 'mate' to Frank Leonard. But then he always offered some service that Leonard needed. 'You want 'im topped?' He cut his own throat with a finger.

Leonard suddenly threw a whole fish at a greedy seagull, broke its wing and sent it flapping into the sea. 'I want him lifted, taken somewhere safe. He's got something I want...'

Tingle threw the dying seagull a scrap or two. 'Here y'are son.' He got up and sicked stomach lining over the side, nothing else left to give. With his shining shaven head, vomitty mouth and broken nose, he was an ugly sight.

Leonard swigged at a can of tonic. 'He's sat tight, done five years like a good boy, now he's going down from category A to B. Out of Wyck Hill over to Garside, thinks life's gonna be soft till he can get out and get at what he's hidden. But we can get at *him* on the road. An' I do want Frenchie Donoghue where I can talk to him.'

Tingle timed it right, but still spat nothing into a wave. 'Yeah, OK, Frank. Be a pleasure.'

'Getting your due always is, Bri.'

They moved in on the hottest day of summer, out of the sticky sweat of Tottenham to where the haze over the marsh had burned itself off, and the shadows of the removal men were the deepest dark as they humped and hoisted furniture into the house.

Sophia had sat silent all the way down. With no air conditioning the car windows were wound fully open and talk was impossible anyway – just the odd shout about the heat, and directions. Sophia and her mother were with Uncle Mike in one car, the Leeds grandparents in another, come down to help with the move.

Car seats face forwards, but it was a journey Sophia should have made facing the other way; she could only look back. Saying goodbye to Eli had been like a death itself, they'd been all through Primary and Comprehensive together and were closer than sisters. They knew every detail of each other's lives – every body measurement, every monthly date, every try a boy had ever made – they could say so much without opening their mouths, thought like one mind; and Sophia knew that right now Eli felt exactly as she did, like a conjoined twin separated from its sibling. They'd said goodbye the night before with tears and kisses and promises of going on seeing each other – trains ran, didn't they, Brighton fans got up to Tottenham for the cup, and these days mobiles and e-mail made Sophia's move less like transportation for life – but these were pathetic attempts at cheering each other up, and they both knew it. Eli had said, '*Shalom! See you in Jerusalem,*' and broken down. It was a real parting – and all for a move that was Sophia's mother's stupid, urgent priority. Lesley Micheli, who was so sick in the head with her hatred of London life that some marshland house at the back of beyond had to be a new, rural venture: and one that Sophia Micheli had to go along with – totally against her will.

Today I left my life behind,
My friend, my streets, my city kind,
The cracks in my pavement, the tags on my wall,

My place in the class, El's smile when I call.
I'm turning my back on the places you knew,
The city you came to, the place where I grew—
It's criminal to slam the door
On everything that's gone before.
Today I left my life behind—
My dad, my streets, my city kind.

B and B, a Bed and Breakfast by the sea. With all those bird-watchers and walkers in the remote area, it couldn't fail – so the estate agent said; it made so much sense, Mrs Micheli. Her work would be at home, there'd be other people in the house a lot of the time, and plenty of opportunity for her own painting – which he was sure would be thrilling under the Kent light; the previous owner had added a very commodious conservatory. Plus, madam, King's Meadows Girls' Grammar school in Folkestone has a very good reputation...

Not even so much as a boy at the school.

Sophia had a bedroom up under the tiles on the second floor. There were three dormer windows in the roof, looking out across the marsh towards the sea; two of them in Lesley's bigger room, the third in Sophia's at the original, eastern end. Which was big enough, because the house was deep as well as wide, and even with the slope of the roof, there was still plenty of head room. It was private, too, with its own back stairs from a door in the kitchen, which was a plus. The staircase to Lesley's ran up centrally from the hallway inside the front door, past the first landing – which had four rooms off – and up to the second floor, narrowing just a bit on the final turn: so she and her mother were on the same floor – but their ways to bed were by different routes. In London it would have been great – creeping in and out with Eli!

Up here at the back of the house was the bathroom and lavatory she and her mother would share through a little interconnecting corridor, while two of the main bedrooms on the floor below had en-suite bathrooms already – and Uncle Mike's builders were coming down to put partitioned plumbing in the others. It was all of a style – unlike the added on conservatory and the ground-floor kitchen at the east end of the house, with the cellar beneath it and the small spare room above it, sharing Sophia's stairs. These rooms had the old *Revenge* in them: the black, solid, shiny timbers, thick going up and middling going across; rough cut in places, with newer nail holes where horse brasses had hung; older screw holes for hammocks; and cracks filled with black pitch to keep out the sea water.

But Lesley wasn't going to give the place its original name, whatever some local character had said.

'Who'd want B and B in a place called Revenge House?'

'Dunno – they're a sad lot, bird-watchers.'

'Marsh End suits fine, thank you.'

'Sad, like her!' From up a ladder fixing her end of a curtain, Sophia nodded down at a woman on the road. She was hard to put an age on, young but middle-aged, binoculars in front, backpack behind, and wearing a waterproof cape – crazy for such a hot day. Staring at the eccentric sight, one of the removal men nearly lost his grip on a bookcase. The woman had a word with him, and Sophia caught it, 'London'.

'And she's got a nose on her!'

'It proves they're about, anyhow,' her mother said. 'Bird-watchers. I'll be after her trade in a month or so.' She looked along at Sophia. '*We'll* be after her trade.' She gave it a pause, to sink in. 'Because we're in this together, Sofe. It's you and me.'

There was another silence, a longer one. After the rows, was this when Sophia was supposed to give in, now it was too late? She kept her eyes out of the window, on the distant horizon. There were too many helpers in the house for trouble.

'A bit like *Treasure Island*, eh?' Lesley went on, forcing the upbeat mood.

'A bit. So who have you got me down for? *Jim, lad?*'

'If you like.'

Sophia watched the bird-loving woman go walking off along the road towards the sea. 'Yeah! And it'll be your luck to get some Captain Billy Bones come to stay.'

'Could be *good* luck, that,' Lesley said, 'if he's got a map in his sea chest with a cross on it...'

Sophia looked away, got busy with the curtain because she was crying inside. What Sophia Antonia Micheli had treasured most in life was back in London, one buried, one lost, and her own grieving hadn't started yet.

CHAPTER THREE

Frenchie Donoghue sat in his cell waiting for the prison officer on his landing to take him to the electronics shop to make circuit boards. It was a single cell, one of the 'Ones', because until the move Donoghue was still a category A prisoner. But in there with him this morning was another con also waiting to go to work – a twenty-year-old with a tough face and a twisted smile. He was new, and a Londoner; and new Londoners were always given the once over. In prison, cockneys looked after cockneys, scousers looked after scousers, and jocks looked after themselves, that was what they said. But you had to be OK'd before you got to be a member of the London firm, before anyone would do violence for you against the screws or other cons. You didn't walk into Frenchie's cell for your interview, though – you definitely had to be invited. Come in without the call and he'd snarl, 'Get out! This ain't the Caff de Paris!' He was careful about his associates.

'Yeah, we done the Antwerp job,' Frenchie was saying, 'no secret about that. An' it went like a dream till after.' It sounded as if he were establishing his own credentials, not the other way around; but then, new faces had to know not to mess with the really big boys.

'An' they never found nothing?' the Smile asked. 'They never got it back?'

Frenchie stared him out, then shook his head. 'Nah, never did. It's stashed somewhere over France, they reckon. God knows where, or who had it away, I know I never. They done me for hitting the guard, hard – came lookin' an' took DNA off me, said the same match was all over the geezer – so that's my ten stretch.'

'Manslaughter.'

'Accident.'

'Now you're gettin' put down to a B an' being shanghaied.'

'Prison's prison, i'n it, wherever it is?'

The new man looked away and at the door. 'So no one's got a map o' France with a cross on it nowhere, then?' Still the smile, like a knife slash.

Frenchie took in a series of breaths through his nostrils, said nothing.

'Then why do they call you Frenchie?'

The older con took in more snorts of stale air,

heavy with the morning smells of men's bowels. Breathing in deep was what you learnt not to do in prison. 'Not that it's none of your business, son, but my ol' lady worked over Disney, I was always over Paris…'

'So you do know the lie of the land…?'

'Like you know Plaistow an' Wormwood Scrubs.' Donoghue's breathing *was* getting deeper.

'They could have called you…Walt! Walt Disney!' The smile was a cheeky fraction too wide, while his eyes told the older con that he could have said Mickey Mouse instead.

'Frenchie to you – an' I tell you what – you call me anythink else, son, an' I'll have your ears for Wrigleys.'

The Smile looked at him again. He saw what the prison saw, the sleek black hair, the drawn skin around brown eyes like someone who's had a new face, and those white teeth – fifty looking thirty-five: and disturbing because the man's stare was always held so still.

With a sudden jangle and a stamp of boots Davies the landing screw came into the doorway. 'Right,' he said, 'youse two, get to your work.'

The Smile stayed sitting, defiant. But Frenchie Donoghue stood up straightaway. 'Right you are, guv'nor' – for all the world like someone keeping his nose clean; biding his time patiently. 'Get up an' get out!' he told the new man, kicking at the man's boot. 'This ain't the Caff de Paris!' And they went through to the electronics shop where, on the way, they got a glimpse of the sky.

In the paddock behind Marsh End Lesley Micheli walked a full three-sixty degrees with her face up to the same sky. In the distance to the east a low line of hills marked the North Downs, otherwise nothing for miles around reached any higher towards heaven than the trees.

'Toni,' she whispered as if he were the sun, 'Toni.'

Sophia was in the timbered kitchen, looking out. She knew what her mother was doing, *worshipping* being where she was – and she turned away in disgust. Never mind the *Revenge* and Nelson, this was Napoleon Bonaparte stuff – *exile*. Stuck away out here! You had to live your life with *people* – your own people, in streets, communities, towns, cities – not shoot off to some open-air prison with the sky for walls.

Sophia shook her head at a family picture; a happy family picture taken in their small Tottenham back garden. She knew *why* her mother had done it, but *how* could she? Knowing and understanding are two different things. Lesley Micheli's professional life had been in the thrust and thrill of designing arena and theatre stages and sets – producers, bands, performers – a career on the up, rushing here, rushing there, a train to Manchester to see an opening; a bollocking for a scenery dock for getting a colour wrong; almost with the clout to tell Cameron Mackintosh what he could and couldn't have in this size venue or that; all 'get-ins' and 'get-outs' and 'techs' and 'dress runs', flies and prosses and revolves. She was always in and out of the house at a run with a portfolio or a model set, waving a mobile phone so hot she put it in the fridge at night. Small, athletic – people asked her what sport she did, which was none – and a voice that had you jumping whether you were a director, a stage manager, a barman – or a daughter.

And all this – everything that drove her by the strength of her own adrenalin – she was giving up to lift her face to the country sun.

After Rome she'd met Sophia's dad again, working on *Guys and Dolls* for the British tour. They'd got the video, it was Sophia's favourite. And what did Guy Masterson always sing in the show? 'My Time of Night,' the life of New York in the early hours, the *real* life. Sophia went along with that: life should be *when* you live it as well as *where,* and imagine anything happening down here after nine p.m.! Her mother had turned her back on everything she'd known and everything Sophia had treasured to make them live like hermits on the marshes. And no debate! No say for her! As a kid you walked where your parents walked, ran where your parents ran, loved who they loved and hated who they hated. You didn't question any of it, because you were part of it. But as you got older your loves and hates changed, and some even turned inward on you – especially two people with wills so strong that they could never agree. Perhaps that was why it wasn't discussed, why it was only ever quarrelled over. Never mind Sophia having a life and a best friend and interests of her own, never mind her being taller than her mother and capable of having her own children – Lesley had decided they'd move, so they both moved.

Holiday, OK. Sophia would go along with that, a bit of peace and quiet for a fortnight's change: a drop of sun and the smell of Piz Buin, good for a couple of hours at a go, on the beach or in the mountains up behind Alássio where her dad had come from, short walks to old ruins – great. It was the night time Sophia liked best, the promenading up and down the front, knots of kids, the seeing and being seen; the Cokes in crowded cafés, and the talk, and the rev of small engines. Especially her dad with a crowd of his old school mates, his *amicos*, and the kissing and the laughs – what she'd been looking forward to at Club

Seventeen with Eli and Jon Elite and had tasted just the once. Instead of which it was her and her mum out here for good, and soon our little feathered friends being stalked and talked about by gabby old walkers who'd be living with them in their house.

Sophia looked away from the picture, across the kitchen at the new dishwasher that had come; the commercial job for Bed and Breakfasts, tucked into an old fireplace under a heavy *Revenge* beam. Bought with promised death money, like the house itself – an upgrade on the old mortgage – with the en-suite bathrooms and the breakfast furniture all paid for by her dad's insurance and the criminal compensation money awarded against the hit and run drug dealer they'd caught.

That slimy slug! What he'd done to their lives! Sophia looked back out at her slender mum, arms up in the early summer sun, kidding herself she was content. Perhaps coming here took the worst edge off her hatred for the people who'd killed Toni Micheli – the pushy, clubbing girls and that criminal driver – but it couldn't work for ever, no medicine ever could...

And there and then, blinking out into the sunshine, with the same strong inherited will as her mother, Sophia decided that this wasn't going to last for ever: definitely not any longer than it had to – not if she had anything to do with it. And in that moment just having an aim made Sophia feel a little bit better. She took in a big, decisive breath.

She heard a voice in the garden; not her mother's but a voice she'd heard before – and voices here were rare. It was Fred Kiff, the odd-job man who'd told Sophia about Revenge House the day they'd come to see it.

'Morning, Missus.' The old man lifted the cap as brown as his face to show a bald, white head to the sky. 'Any jobs you're wanting done?' He was pushing a bike with a barrow latched on behind. In it Sophia could see an old sack and shears, cutters and a shovel.

'Hi!' Her mother was smiling at the old man, no doubt somewhere over the rainbow with this rustic character who fitted into her country dream. 'What do you do?'

'I was along before. Told your girl about old Revenge House.'

'Marsh End. I know. You're Mr Kiff.'

The old man smiled.

'So, what *do* you do?'

His smile held straight as he waved his hand at the very obvious gardening gear in his barrow. 'I do a bit of sea fishing, brain surgery, com-puter construction an' internet trading.'

Sophia heard her mother laugh, but not very hard.

Was her Old Masters' painting of the countryside flaking a bit?

'No, seriously.'

'Whatever you want, Missus. Jobs around the place. I'm off up to the Manor House now. I can give a lick o' paint where you want it, or drop a drip o' number seven on your hinges. That small sort o' stuff. Or I can get you what you want a bit cheap – fish of course, wine, spirits, 'cept you're not doing meals, are you?'

Lesley shook her head.

'I've got your real sign in my yard. I could fix it back for you, give the place its proper name.'

'Thanks, but we're all right for jobs right now. I'll see how we go.'

Fred Kiff doffed his cap again. 'Best way. Count your lambs afore you call the shearers in. So I'll bid you good day for the present.' And he pushed his bike on, suddenly stopping and turning his head to smile again. 'I'll come back quicker, downhill.'

He was explaining why he wasn't cycling but pushing – although so far as Sophia could tell there was no gradient in the road whatever.

Lesley's second thoughts came five minutes later. She called to Sophia as she pulled a dozen dishcloths from the plastic lines of the rotary dryer. 'Sofe – do us a favour, will you?'

'Leave home? Do us both a favour?'

No reaction. 'Catch up that man, Mr Kiff. Ask him to call in when he's coming back.'

'Why?'

'Because he can fix our proper washing line – over to the barn.' The brick-ended outbuilding was about thirty metres from the house. 'I won't get many sheets and towels on this thing.'

'I can climb up there.'

'But you can't Rawlplug a hook and pulley to the wall.'

'If he reckons that road's uphill, he'll never climb a ladder. Tell me about Rawlplugs.' There was nothing happened without an argument.

'Ask him. Or you can make a start on the ironing...'

'I'll ask him,' Sophia said, going for the gate.

'Head for the Manor House. That's what he said.'

'I know, I heard.' And Sophia went.

With her longer legs she had the advantage on old Fred Kiff, pushing his bike and barrow. The sun was on her face as she went, her half Mediterranean skin continental already. What shone out were her blue eyes which, with short barbered hair, gave her the look of an up for anything Ariel; which she would have been, given half the chance. Up for anything.

The narrow road twisted, went where the stream

meandered, but it didn't divide. Looking back Sophia could see the tall chimneys of Marsh End above the ivy clutched trees. Looking ahead she couldn't see any Fred Kiff; he must have come to the top of his flat hill and got on his bike. But suddenly pointing a decision for her on the opposite side to the stream was a signpost in the hedgerow, leading off to a footpath across the fields: a wooden hand and arm and a chiselled name – Middle Marsh Manor.

So she could cut him off, catch him before he went in if she was lucky. She took the footpath; or rather, the footpath took her. It went where the hedge went, with fields of long barley on one side and prickly bush on the other, and she had to follow its slow dance even though she could see the high wall and chimneys of a house straight ahead across the crop. The path was hardly a path at all, overgrown with stingers on one side – and Sophia wished she'd got socks or boots instead of bare legs.

Twist and turn, but the wall and chimneys came nearer – close enough for Sophia to see their small red Elizabethan bricks. There wasn't any doubt; it had to be the manor house Fred Kiff was heading for; she'd passed it in the car going to the shop at St Mary-in-the-Marsh and there was nothing else like it around. And that was some wall! It was as tall as a prison's, except keeping people out, not in, probably with some fat old lord or tall skinny duchess living it up on the other side.

She was nearly there – and she'd have to rush this last corner of field if she was going to beat Fred Kiff to it. She turned a trot into a run – and nearly screamed her head off as the barley on her left suddenly parted and something rose up into the air like a frightened beast.

'Mary, Mother of God!'

'Sorry!' A beast which didn't moo, baa, bark or bite but spoke – a person, camouflaged in a green cape; a woman under a wide safari hat, with binoculars in her hands. It was that weird bird-watcher they'd seen before, outside the house when they'd moved in, younger up close, and with unblinking eyes.

'Who frightened who?' the woman asked. 'I wasn't reckoning on anything bigger than a pigeon.'

'I wasn't reckoning on anything at all!' Sophia breathed hard, blew out her scare.

The bird-watcher stayed crouching. 'In some sort of a rush?' She was keeping her voice low.

'Could be...' If it was any business of hers.

'At Middle Marsh?'

Sophia nodded. She couldn't hang about being secretive. 'I'm after the odd-job man...'

'Ah... Well, keep quiet about me, this might be one of their fields.'

Sophia looked at the manor house. She could see its gates from here, so anyone looking out would see her talking to someone; or hear them; definitely hear them. It was so quiet right now that a sound in the sky had her looking up at a small brown bird hovering over the field, trilling a few notes, beautiful, but sad.

The woman followed her look. 'Skylark,' she said.

'Yeah,' said Sophia, leaving her to it. And on she went, along the hedge and over a stile to the road, right opposite the gates of Middle Marsh Manor. Up close they looked huge, as tall as the wall – and she'd been wrong, no one could have seen her through them because behind the wrought-iron design there was studded wood, painted black, filling the gates in. It was just like one of her mother's stage sets that gave the look of deep distance without showing anything.

And Sophia was lucky. Along the road, pedalling slowly, came Fred Kiff.

'Whoa back!' At the second attempt he cocked his leg over the crossbar and stood at the gate.

'She changed her mind,' Sophia said. 'She's got a job for you after all.'

'Ah.' He smiled. 'She wants her proper sign put up?'

'No, a clothes line. From the barn to the wall.'

Fred Kiff pushed at a button on the gate's key

plate. Something rasped. 'Kiff,' he said into the grill –
and the gates gave a clunk, ready to be pushed open.
'Tell her I'll drop by an' have a look.'

'OK.'

'I'm happy wi' low heights, if that don' sound
French.' He looked up at the same bird, still trilling
its sad song over the barley. 'A woodlark I ain't.'

Sophia laughed: well, old men expected a laugh
after a joke. She said goodbye and took the road back
towards Marsh End; but not too fast. She still didn't
fancy the ironing.

CHAPTER FOUR

Bev Leonard had made the mistake of forgetting that Fred Kiff was coming – or she hadn't been told. She'd gone out into the walled garden of Middle Marsh Manor wearing only a short silk dressing gown. One swish as she threw burnt toast at the birds and she could have shocked the old man – except he was by the gate doing some business with her husband, giving him something from his sack.

Frank Leonard looked up. 'You showing yourself again?' He grabbed the patio door and pulled it locked shut behind him. Now she'd have to stay as she was in the garden or climb in through a conservatory window. Either way shaming.

But she knew better than to whine at what he'd done. She held herself tall. 'Where you going?'

'Not far.' Leonard dismissed Fred Kiff and went round to the front of the house where his Mercedes was waiting with the engine running quietly, cooling its interior. He drove out of the electronic gates and turned left, heading south across the marsh.

When he'd gone Bev tried the patio door, just in case it hadn't locked; but it had. She looked for an open window, but the only one at all likely would need a leg up to climb through. Head up high, she called Fred Kiff over before he went, too.

'Would you treat your dog like this?' she asked him.

'Haven't got a dog, missus.'

'Have you got A levels?'

The old man looked perplexed. He shook his head.

'I have!' Bev told him. 'Three. Could have gone to university but I fell for the high life. Money, respect, luxury and comfort my family had never known – and nothing Frank wouldn't do for me. Once. And now this!' She lifted the patio window. 'Down to getting a bunk up from an old man to get back into my own house.'

'Don' worry about that. I'll bend over, make a back.'

Which he did; and whether he was smiling or not, Bev Leonard wouldn't know; she was landing inside as elegantly as she could.

Leonard himself was soon at the Nelson in Sandgate, a long narrow pub whose back door stepped out into the heaped shingle of the beach – the entrance he used. He was in trainers, jeans and a silk magenta shirt, could have been in Spain had his skin not been cold white.

In the back a strong-armed local girl was plumbing a tube to a beer keg.

'Tell 'im I'm here,' Leonard commanded.

She didn't look up. 'Tell him *who's* here?'

With the sole of his trainer Leonard kicked the keg off its cradle, thudding it full to the ground and bouncing beer all over the girl; her hair, her face, her vest, her Bermudas.

'Tell 'im *I'm* here.'

Wiping herself she hurried through to the front bar where the landlord was checking his spirits.

'There's a rough stuff out the back says he's here.'

He looked her up and down. 'He done that?'

She nodded.

'That all? You're lucky! Watch the bar.' The guv'nor, Terry Ford, lifted the flap and went through to the back – tall with grey hair trimmed in the West End, one of those film and TV faces no one can name, but is seen in every gangster movie made.

Leonard was out on the beach, sitting on the shingle and throwing stones at seagulls. Ford crunched over and sat next to him.

'She needs a slapping, that girl,' Leonard said.

'Denise? She'll get one! She's new!'

'I don't want no mistakes this end. This is s'posed to be the easy bit.'

'And there won't be any, Frank. It's all set. Room at the back for the man, no one passing except the gulls. Hair dye, wardrobe, shoes, all organised; television but no 'phone; me an' my friend' – he tapped his pocket – 'rooms for your minders, everything you ordered.'

Frank Leonard pulled on his sunglasses against the glare. 'That's all right, then.' He looked round at Terry Ford. 'You can play me in the film.'

Ford laughed. 'Except they'll never make it, Frank – because they won't know, will they?'

'You're right.'

'You got the plane organised?' Ford asked.

A sudden chill seemed to roll in off the sea. Leonard stood up, took off his shades and stared down at the actor-landlord. 'You jus' organise this end, an' don't get into nothing else. I want 'im laid low while things cool off, held tight, that's your brief.'

'Sure, Frank. No problems.'

'An' there ain't better be.' One word out of place and Leonard's claws were out sharp.

Terry Ford got up, too. He always had his height over Frank Leonard. 'Any idea when? I do need to know that.'

'Yeah, I'll tell you when. When it happens. You

know my phones, they sell tickets to listen in. I've only come to tell you it's on, it's a "go". You'll know when – when I come an' tell you.'

'Fine.' Terry Ford cocked his head. 'Want a drink before you go?'

'Who said I'm going?' But Leonard did. He turned about in a scrape of shingle and walked off along the beach to where the glinting sea met the road.

The glint in Fred Kiff's grey eyes was more twinkle now – definitely so. He came whistling down the road to Marsh End with his feet stuck out in front and his tool cart rattling behind.

Using a long extension lead from the conservatory Lesley was ironing tea towels in the shade beneath an oak tree, not quite singing but looking as if she might.

Sophia heard Fred Kiff's arrival from her dormer room up high, just coming off the internet and an e-mail from Eli – who'd been to Club Seventeen where Jon Elite had been asking after Sophia. And, yes, he was using Sophia's name for him now; he fancied it! If Sophia rang Eli on her mobile she'd give her all the details! But with that news Sophia felt more cut off from things than her poor dead dad; and right now the last thing she wanted to do was to ring London. She shut the computer down with a thump at her mouse and went downstairs to get out of the house. There was no comfort in here.

In the garden Fred Kiff was squinting his eye into the space between the barn and the house.

'Don't say it's too high,' Sophia interrupted. She could climb it, she only needed a Rawlplug.

'About my limit,' the old man said. He looked at Lesley. 'I charge vertical, not horizontal. She's right, it's going up'll cost you, not the across.'

'That's OK. When can you do it?'

'Not today, wouldn't be safe. 'Ad my eyesight strained this morning. Tomorrer.'

'Looking at that lark?' Sophia cut in. 'Are they a strain to tell apart?' That bird-watcher woman had reckoned it was a skylark. 'Woodlark, you said?' She didn't really give a toss but it was something to say in the marsh boredom.

'Birds ain't just eyesight, girl, they're ear'oles an' all.' And he whistled the three note call of the bird they'd seen. 'Sad an' be-ootiful, that's your woodlark, that's what you heard.'

'You know birds?' Lesley asked.

'Not much I haven't seen in my time.' Fred Kiff pouted his lips and blinked his eyes.

'Do you get many bird people come to the marsh?'

'You trip over 'em sometimes, Missus.'

Sophia snorted. That was true enough.

'So an advert in a bird-watcher magazine would

pay off, for a guest house?' Lesley asked.

'I should reckon.' He suddenly slapped his leg – as if now he understood. 'Ah! That's why you don't want ol' Revenge House, I see it. Sounds more like murders in the dark than muffins round the fire, don' it?'

'It do,' said Lesley – and Sophia snorted again; her mother falling into country talk so soon! It was pathetic – but the sort of thing her dad would laugh at when he came home. And she caught herself with a choke; because he wouldn't come home any more, he wasn't away on tour with stories to hear when he came swinging through the door. It was a diabolical trick the mind could play, like in the dreams she had where he was still alive. There'd be no more laughs with him – not with anyone. He was dead in his grave, worlds away back in London.

'So we'll see you tomorrow?' Lesley asked Fred Kiff.

'You will. You got a ladder.'

'I don't know.'

'That's not a question, Missus, you have. In your barn. Can't say what time.'

'Don't worry,' Lesley said. 'We're not going anywhere.'

Which was so true it hurt, Sophia thought, as Fred Kiff went off on his bike with a bit of extra push to his legs.

It was all to do with diamonds, Sophia was told, yawn, yawn! Bed and Breakfasts. If you want to get on the recommended lists you have to have diamonds from the English Tourist Council: one, two, three, four or five; and Lesley Micheli was aiming for the full necklace as soon as possible. She'd helped design West End theatre sets and Number One tours, political conferences and rock shows, she was used to working at the top. Now Sophia knew she'd be top at this God-awful boring job.

The walls, linen, furniture and pictures in the four double rooms said Manet or Monet or Degas or Renoir. The one single was the spare room beneath Sophia's which was opened up as the Turner, with a picture above the bed of what could have been the old *Revenge* in the sunset. It gave Sophia no joy, but for a surprise Lesley painted the ceiling white with spots of fluorescence hidden in, invisible in the daytime but which glowed in the dark like the starry heavens at night, for the room to steer itself by. All this, she reckoned, gave those extra somethings that five diamonds would require.

'Wow!' Jenny was very impressed – Jennifer Barton from Sophia's new school. She lived in Dymchurch and they'd met on the first bus home. Tonight she'd come out on her bike pretending to talk about homework but right now she was inspecting one of the en-suite bathrooms. 'You want to get this opened by the Queen.'

'She's busy this month. Balmoral, love.'

'Get Prince William. Yeah!'

'Yeah!'

They both nodded hard at the thought of that.

She was no Eli, there could never be another Eli – old friends take years to grow – but some new friendships can start with a straight-off spark: two people meeting up by chance and there's laughter or danger or just being thrown into the same box of fireworks together - and Jenny was a sudden life-saver.

Up to the start of term the whole marsh thing could have been just summer holiday – everyone splits, even Sophia and Eli going their different ways – then September brings reality back; it's into school again and new looks and old laughs. But not for Sophia, not this year. She knew who *wouldn't* be waiting for her on the corner, so the night before term began she'd given her new uniform a good kicking round her bedroom: starting a new school was never going to be a bundle of fun, but there was no need to go in looking a sprog. And all through her first day at King's Meadows Girls' Grammar the same thought had filled her head. *This is where I am now, till the day I can bring the rotten house crashing down!* It could have been worse, Sophia knew. She wasn't a refugee, living in a council B and B – her mother *owned* one. She wasn't black, down here on Kent's white coast – she was an olive-skinned Anglo-Italian. She wasn't fat or disfigured – she was a good-looking girl. So she was one of those for whom life isn't so complicated. Except losing a dear dad still squeezed her heart as dry as used citrus.

And so had Jenny, it turned out – lost a dad – although hers had gone off to live with someone else, he'd *chosen* to abandon her. She was in Sophia's year, not her form, but they were the only two King's Meadows girls going home on the Romney bus that first day; suddenly pulled together against two local Comprehensive boys who got on at Hythe. These two headed for the seat behind Jenny and started on at her; it could have been a regular buzz for them, winding up the Grammar girl. Sophia watched it from the back of the bus.

'Want a snog?' one of them asked. Jenny kept her stare fixed out of the window at the sea – good for her. Then he leant over her seat back and stared down her shirt. 'What did the boy say to the girl when he put his hand down her top?'

Jenny did well, kept up the ignoring out of the window – but apart from Sophia there was only an elderly couple on the bus and they were busy going over their Safeway's till roll; the driver busy with the road and having a quiet smoke. So the kid persisted. 'Eh? He said, "I feel a right tit, doing this!"' Snigger, snort, snigger.

Already, wearing the same school uniform made Sophia feel an ally of the girl being harassed. And she and Eli used to eat kids like this one for morning break. He was dribbling on about bra cups and Jenny only needing saucers when Sophia suddenly got up from her seat and walked down the bus to stand in the aisle next to him.

'Erk!' she said in a loud voice. 'What *have* you done in your trousers, little boy?'

The Safeway's till roll was suddenly forgotten. The bus driver looked back at them, swerved. The second kid punched the first and sneered, so much for loyalty. The foul-mouthed boy swore at Sophia standing over him, suddenly got up himself, went for the door and rang the bell for the bus to stop. The other followed and they jumped off quickly, mouthing and apeing while the bus pulled away. 'Thanks!' said Jenny.

'No prob!'

'Big men! You know they're our age?'

'And their voices haven't broken!'

'Anyhow, you scared him stiff!'

'Or the opposite!' At which the two of them laughed till they were nearly sick, the old Eli touch.

Jenny was shorter than Sophia, with long auburn hair and freckles. When she went red she boiled – on the bus she'd gone like a ceramic hot plate – so there was no way people *wouldn't* know when she was flustered or upset, or what sort of thing she was thinking. Unlike Eli, who could con a psychologist.

'I hate it!' Jenny told Sophia. 'I'm transparent!' But it didn't stop her from putting her foot in it all the time.

That first evening at Marsh End she suddenly asked Sophia's mother how she'd feel about being all alone in the house with a man.

'How do you mean?' Lesley asked sharply. And Sophia straightened. This question wasn't completely off the wall; it was just one of those that their rows had avoided – though God knew why, it was a stupid thing her mother hadn't thought through.

In the en-suite Lesley was deciding how she was going to hang her towels: invent her house style.

'Well, what if a guest was dead gorgeous and he was lying in bed?'

Lengthwise, the towel went, hanging down from the rail, not along it. 'I won't do singles. Not if I can help it.'

'But it could happen.'

'I wouldn't see him in bed. There's no reason I'd be

in his room till after breakfast is cleared and he's gone out. "Dead gorgeous" or not!' No, along, not down. Lesley made a move to get out of the small room.

'Or what if you're on your own and he tries something on? After breakfast?'

'I'd tell him to get lost – bloody quick!'

'Yes. Sorry. Just wondered.' Jenny's face and neck warmed the room better than any heater. 'Only, it's what my dad did with some hotel lady somewhere: so they say.' All the same, she'd hit on a real danger – with Lesley alone out here on the marshes when Sophia was at school; or even with the two of them in the house at Marsh End. Out and out crooks weren't the only men you had to fear – and ugly customers like that didn't limit themselves to the cities.

But Jenny was definitely someone good to have around, a consolation for missing Eli big time – except that Jenny would go on wishing she could sleep over when the first visitors came so she could be one of the team. Sophia was going to have to do some straight talking to her, getting all 'B and B' with her mother! It wasn't going to help to get this nonsense stopped.

She really couldn't understand the crazy thinking of the woman – wanting to live a humdrum, day in day out *housemaid's* existence, about as glamorous as serving passengers on a plane – instead of being part of the London, show biz, no two days alike, vibrant life she'd left. Quarrelling with her mother was no good, she never got any real answers, always the same 'had to get out of London' crap. But every night Sophia thought about it. She asked the Madonna on her dressing table to give her understanding. But she got no joy from her, either, so she talked to her father – wherever he was – and every night she cried her unhappiness into her pillow. If Lesley Micheli thought that *her* life had moved on after the death of her husband, it hadn't for Sophia, after the death of her father. Not underneath it hadn't.

It hadn't moved on, and it didn't move back. Through e-mail and mobile phone she and Eli fixed a date, a marvellous Saturday when Eli was coming down to see her. Definitely. She was coming to Hythe Station and Sophia was meeting her there and bringing her back to Dymchurch on the miniature railway that ran from Hythe to Romney; they'd walk home to Marsh End across the fields catching up and sharing the old sayings. Jenny had to be put off, but mixing old and new friendships wouldn't be a good idea, not when the new is very new and the old is at the other end of a very long thin thread. So Sophia got everything ready, made sure they had Eli's favourite lasagne, planned an afternoon roaming round where their fancies took them, talking, talking,

talking; and she put on a discreet amount of make-up so that Eli could tell Jon Elite what a cracker she still was!

And it was only ten minutes before Sophia left for the little train in to Hythe that Eli rang. Her father wouldn't let her come: the south coast was too far away for her to travel on her own. She could come another time when his business was this way and he could bring her.

It was the depth, the pit of unhappiness for Sophia. She took the message on the phone in the kitchen and ran back to her room to wipe her tears round her face with a pillowcase, smearing her sophistication. Here she was, a blubbering kid, and tonight, Saturday night, Eli would be at Club Seventeen again with the others! How far away could you feel? How deeply cut off? How *desperate* for what you've once had?

And her mother hadn't even followed her upstairs to give her any consolation. She was outside taking advantage of the sunshine to peg the washing on Fred Kiff's line. Singing, no doubt! Her down there and Sophia up here.

But what was the point of bloody *bemoaning*? Sophia came away from the window, sobbing but now there was the tremble of a decision in her breast. What was the point of doing anything except taking direct action? If she wanted away, back to London, then why should she wait till she was old enough to leave home or go to university? She was going to do something about it now! And there might be a way, short of setting fire to the house...

Pulling herself under control, Sophia checked again that her mother was in the garden, before creeping out of her room and along the old landing to the new part of the house. She came to her mother's dormer bedroom and with a last check, still making weird chokes at the end of her upset, she went inside and over to Lesley's bedside table. Nervously, like opening a window into her mother's heart, she pulled open the drawer. She didn't want to see anything secret, she didn't want to know anything widow personal, but she did want to get hold of her mother's 'book', that special Filofax with all the dates and the contacts that theatricals carry.

And it was there. Swiftly, Sophia found the entry for her agent, the woman who got Lesley Micheli all her work. She memorised the phone number and replaced the book, made sure it went back exactly where it had come from. Hurrying out of the room, suddenly more noisy and confident as she went back to her own, she shut her door and locked it and fished for her mobile phone. And she rang Lesley's agent's personal weekend number and told her how as a daughter, she reckoned her mother

65

would react to a really good offer.

The sort of offer no one with any creativity could refuse. And to remind Lesley Micheli of what she was really about, Sophia pulled out of their cardboard tube theatre posters of the shows she had designed, and Blu-tacked them all around her walls.

CHAPTER FIVE

'So what's the word, guv?' Frenchie Donoghue was carrying his supper into the cell from the landing hot plate: thin mince, chips, soggy cabbage and a small banana on the wrong side of yellow; a mug of tea and a handful of bread.

'What's what word?'

'You know what word. My transfer.'

The landing screw looked down at the tray with its plastic cutlery. 'You won't get better food nowhere else, Frenchie.'

'I won't have to see your eyeball at the peep'ole every time I look.'

'Standard of care. You won't get our standard of care – an' you won't have a private room. You sure you want to go?'

'Too right I am.'

'Well, I don't know when, do I? What makes you think I know?'

''Cos you know everything, Mr Davies.'

'Oh, yes. *Big Book of Knowledge*, I am.' And he banged up Frenchie Donoghue for the night – at five p.m. He saw the Smile and the other Category As into their cells, secured the landing, and went to the Wing Manager's office on the landing below.

'Donoghue's going on about his transfer,' he told him.

'So? Let him sweat. We'll lay it on him on the day, why should he be different?' The Wing Manager was a tall, calm young officer in a very smart shirt – perhaps because he had to change it a lot on account of the spittle on his back.

'He won't want to organise nothing, get sprung,' Davies said, one of the old, seen-everything squad. 'Too much to lose if he does a runner. He wants a quiet three years on category B then he'll go to South America via France and live like a millionaire. *Be* a millionaire.'

The WM eyed him. 'Could be,' he said. 'But that's all guesswork. No one proved he hid the Antwerp stuff. He wouldn't go down to a B if they thought that.' Nevertheless, when the landing screw went, the WM tapped in a code on his computer and read some details off the screen; which he printed out and folded into his pocket.

Mr and Mrs Henderson came first, on the thirteenth of September – a date Sophia had scrawled into her school year book with double the violent underlining she used for the exam timetable - '13/9: <u>UNWANTED GUESTS</u>!' She went to school from the home of the two Michelis and came back to a house of strangers.

The Hendersons were on a fresh start, too: just retired from teaching with tangy leather luggage and matching binoculars that had to be leaving presents. They kept saying 'Ah!' and looking at one another as if they'd found salvation, talked about the RSPB as if it was a new religious order and their *Book of British Birds* was the Bible. Sophia hated them for the way they kept celebrating getting to where her parents had had no chance to get – retirement together. She caught them with their door open, entwined and sighing at the Manet room, which they kept calling Monet, so even Sophia's mother had a twist to her professional smile.

'Had their dinner in Hythe then came in talking *plumage*,' Sophia told Jenny. 'Bet they couldn't tell a pigeon from a paraglider!'

'They would if it poo'd on 'em!'

But Sophia did get a chance for a small victory. As she was heading for the kitchen with a science textbook, the female of the species popped her head out of the dining room, saw the book and said, 'Bad luck, pet! *Devoir*?'

'*Si*,' said Sophia, '*compiti a casa*.'

'Sorry?'

'That's Italian for homework. Yet another language for you!' *You want to talk foreign, Bird Woman, I'm your girl. I'll always have two and a half litres of Italian blood in me!* She smiled and the woman smiled, but Sophia meant hers – a smile of small victory, and small victories would be like meat in the gruel of this new life. Next morning Lesley said she hadn't slept at all in the run up to cooking her first professional breakfast, she'd broken yolks all night in her dreams and got through a couple of dozen eggs in her attempts to fry Mr Henderson a perfect sunny side up. But Sophia had slept. She'd had a consolation prize to whisper to her pillow.

The Hendersons were booked in for three nights – and Jenny wanted like mad to come to inspect them, to be around on the staff side of Marsh End, go through the door marked Private, fill pepper pots or fold napkins into butterflies. 'It's only origami.' After Eli's let-down Jenny was a growing friend and Sophia was tempted, but she decided against, none of this had to be *fun* – this Bed and Breakfast rubbish had to fail. Lesley Micheli was as tense as a first night. *Serves you right – you've dragged us here for this,* now *wave your arms at the sun!* But Sophia couldn't watch it all happening. On the second night she got on her bike and took off with her homework to Jenny's. There she'd get a bit of peace. But what she got was something else. There she met the brother Jenny hadn't mentioned having.

Sol Barton worked for Digital South, putting the latest technology into homes and businesses from Dover to Hastings; nineteen years old with a Honda he rode like a bull which needed taming. He came roaring in from work and sat Sophia up straight with surprise – past the window, parked up, in through the front door and into the living room as if he belonged. Who was this? Sophia lost her grip on her Bic.

'Oh, my brother Sol.' Jenny introduced him as if he were a stray dog who'd come in one day and stayed. 'Sophia from school.'

He must have taken after his father because he wasn't in the fair-skinned, auburn range of Jenny and her mother. His hair was dark and long – longer than Sophia's crop – and his face the same sharp as his mother's but tanned with blue eyes.

'Hi!'

'Hi!'

Sophia and Sol nodded at each other – followed by that non-blink moment of awkward eyes before Sophia went back to the homework. Sol pointed at the French grammar the girls were sharing at the living room table.

'*Devoir?*' he asked.

'*Oui, monsieur.*' Sophia smiled to herself. Small victories came in different forms – most brothers went straight on through to the kitchen to get at the bread.

'*Devoir?* French?' Jenny sneered at him. 'You wouldn't know a bidet from a duvet—'

'I would!'

'—And he's got the wet bed to prove it!'

Which had even Jenny's mother cracking her face through the kitchen doorway.

'Have you eaten, Sophia?'

'No, Mrs Barton – but…'

'Egg and chips.' Which she was cooking out there as if there was nothing so pressing and important in the world. 'There's enough for you.'

'She wouldn't eat chips,' Sol said, 'look at her, this one's a caviar and lettuce girl.'

And the way he said it, not taking a blink as he stared, suddenly stirred Sophia in a Jon Elite Club Seventeen sort of way; which she definitely didn't like. But she stayed for the meal, it was an extra half hour away from Marsh End – although she was pleased that Sol wasn't eating with them, he'd got an evening's overtime to do; flirty compliments gave her indigestion. So Jenny talked for Britain, Mrs Barton sat silent while she focused on each forkful, and Sophia chewed on the fact that she'd have to eat all over again at home so as not to get a row off her mother.

Which she couldn't imagine happening here. Everyone compared mothers, Sophia reckoned. Some girls you envied, others you pitied. Jenny's mother was tall and serious, and by all but ignoring Sophia, seemed to accept her as if she'd known her all her life. Hardly bothering to ask, she'd poured Sophia a coffee as soon as she'd got there. She was a Social Security officer, nine-to-five in Ashford, drove an old Astra, and got on with the day's domestic work in the evenings – not much to say, no radio on, no television, just the look of being intent on nothing but the ironing or the cooking or the tidying. After a grunt at the bidet joke she went quiet, didn't talk to any of them but got on and left them to do the same. So did you envy that – not being pulled this way and that by the likes of Lesley Micheli who had to have life lived her way? Would you love the sort of mother more who was letting good old routine heal the wounds? And where did love between any of them come into things anyway? You took that for granted, it was what you grew up with, the parent being there.

But there'd been something else between Sophia and Lesley ever since Sophia had hit puberty, them being so much alike – a sort of rivalry of wills. It wasn't jealousy over Sophia's dad but just a needing to be the winner over things: like what Sophia wore, what she ate, who her friends were, and where she was and wasn't allowed to go. And those rows were always loud, slamming affairs – with the look of real dislike twisted on each other's faces. But wasn't that because they *cared* enough to quarrel, because they loved each other, mother and daughter…?

Was that true? And if it had been, was it still? Because Sophia felt different now. What her mother had done since Toni Micheli's death had been so over the top, this crass move she'd forced on to Sophia, imposed on her life. Sophia didn't want the London *laughs* any more – who went looking for laughs after what had happened – but why all this *smiling*? Sophia really couldn't stand her mother's forever smiling – all that smugness up at the sky, and that walking round the garden with her arms out as if she were touching at the edges of a new world? *Her* world, Lesley Micheli's, where there was no place for showing any grief.

And Sophia realised with a sick thud inside that part of her hated her mother for it; and then she hated herself for hating.

Do you have to love your mother?
Is it a golden rule?
When she's changed from being who she was

To a matriarchal fool?
The one you fought with, as you do,
But normal, girl with mother—
Before she made your life unreal;
Do you have to love, this other!

Somehow her mother must have known about the meal at Jenny's because when Sophia got home there was no talk of food, just Lesley sitting alone in the visitors' lounge, waiting on the sound of a key in the door from the Hendersons.

'This is the bit I don't like,' she said. 'People out there with a key to our house. You do feel vulnerable...'

You feel a lot of things, Sophia wanted to say. *Have you just woken up to what you're doing?* But she said nothing except good night, with a brush of a kiss and a run up her back stairs to bed, too ashamed of how she felt to linger in the room with her mother.

'So why can't I come?' Jenny wanted to know. 'Doesn't your mum like me?'

''Course not! I mean, of course she does.'

Sophia and Jenny were on the bus home the next day, no schoolboy kids trying anything on.

'Then why not? Just a sleepover Saturday to get

75

the feel of it. I'm wizard with a frying pan!'

Sophia fidgeted this way and that in her seat. She didn't know whether to say it or not – or how to, if she did.

'You've come to us, had a meal, it's a bit one way.' What Jenny thought, Jenny said.

So now Sophia would, too. With a big welling up inside herself, suddenly out it came. 'I'll tell you why not, girl! Because making a B and B a load of bloody fun is totally against my plan!'

'Oooh!' Then, 'I don't get you, Sofe.'

Sophia turned to her new friend and lowered her voice, even in the empty bus. 'Because I want it to be rotten, I want it to fail, I don't want it to go on a day longer than it's got to…'

'Your mum's business?'

Sophia nodded. 'So now you know. My mum's rotten sodding business and my rotten sodding life—'

'Oh, am I in that?' Jenny wanted to know.

'Not that bit of it. But I tell you, girl, I'm going every way about it to close that place down: I'm going to piss in the tea, put spiders in the beds, take the wrong phone messages, I'm going to do whatever it takes. *Then* she'll have to think again. *Then* she'll have to listen to me and look to *my* needs…'

Jenny pulled away, leant into the aisle. 'Whoa!' she

said. 'Hear you! I don't even feel that strong about my dirty dad!'

Sophia put her head down. 'And don't think I don't feel ashamed, either,' she said, 'because I do. But it's her or me, Jen, it's her or me...'

Frank Leonard was talking to a contact who flew in and out of Lydd Airport – Gerald Scott, a pilot who flew in and out of any place where people paid over the odds for stuff they needed badly. He flew guns into the Congo and medicines into Iraq, porn into Bahrein and drink into Dubai. But not usually people; he didn't take passengers. That sort of cargo wasn't space economic; transporting one or two bodies could never pay the same as the equivalent volume of well-packed crates. Unless, of course, it was someone with a good price on their head.

'Ex Cranfield, sir, ex-RAF, ex-British Airways, ex-it and entry, that's my line,' he told Frank Leonard.

Leonard had come to the north Kent Spanish-style villa by taxi from Bromley Station, leaving his car in a Folkestone car park. He covered tracks better than the wind on soft snow, a lesson he'd learnt from being done for murder. 'You know what I want, do you?' he asked the pilot.

'I've been told.'

'So you tell me what you've been told.' Frank

Leonard held his glass of tonic delicately, finger and thumb, like a vicar at a christening.

Gerald Scott knocked back his Scotch and Canada Dry. 'You want a client of yours flown to France, a chappie who's obliged to…er…circumnavigate the usual channels.'

'Talk English, we need to get him over France, secret – while half the country's turned over looking for him.'

The pilot tipped a fresh packet of peanuts into an ashtray and scooped up a handful, crunching noisily and dropping salt down his RAF Club tie. 'Well, I've been thinking about it…'

'Good. I pay for thinking – instead of VAT.'

'The word was, sometime in the middle of October…?'

'It's what I've been told. Sounds good information.'

'…Only, on the weekend of the fifteenth of October there's an air rally down at Lydd – when the South of England weekend pilots have their annual beano over to Le Touquet. Last chance before the clocks go back. Half the small planes south of the Medway go on a jolly to La Belle France, over on Saturday, enjoy a few bevvies and a ton of snails, and back on Sunday afternoon.' Crunch, crunch.

'So?'

'They're all known, sir, all upright citizens, the

immigration chappies at Lydd won't give any of them a second look, them or their sisters or their cousins or their aunts. Besides, since the European Union there are no checks on people leaving the country, only coming back...'

'I said, "So?"'

'Well, yours truly is one of them!' His face opened as if he expected a loop the loop celebration. 'And it's a deal safer than flying out at night – where we'd show up on the radar like a pimple on a beauty queen...'

Leonard stared out of the window. 'You say the Saturday?' He came back. 'That fits. He'll be out the Wednesday before, give us time to do what we want with him and put up a few decoy sightings the other end of the country...'

'I'm sure you've got it perfectly planned...'

'What about the other side?'

'The police?'

'*Over* the other side. The French end?'

Gerald Scott poured himself another stiff one. 'Sweet as a nut. When we land, the gendarmes just ask for the aircraft registration and the number of passengers – no names, no pack drill – and wave us through. Most of our chappies head straight for the airport restaurant.' He rubbed his peanut-oiled hands together, clearly pleased with himself. 'But we just take off again to anywhere you like for a couple of hundred miles, no flight plan necessary: scores of small airfields in northern France where security's one man and a dog…'

'So how d'you find these airfields?'

'GPS, sir.'

'GPS?'

'Satellite navigation. Got one in your car, haven't you?'

'Never use it; I always know where I'm going.' Frank Leonard took another delicate sip of his tonic and cracked his throat with a loud burp. 'Yeah, that sounds OK. You land him at one o' them – to be arranged – an' my firm escorts him on.'

'Going where?' Gerald Scott asked.

'Somewhere a few would like to know – an' you're well down the queue.'

The pilot placated with his hands, smiled. 'I'm trained not to crack under torture, you know…'

'You'd crack under mine, Biggles. Fast.'

And in that moment of threat and awkwardness the deal was done: money was talked and Gerald Scott smiled all the way to his country club to start running up a bill; while Frank Leonard took a devious route back to Middle Marsh Manor to start planning what to do with ten million pounds.

CHAPTER SIX

With the schools back and the holidaymakers gone, the marsh went from quiet to desolate, no cars losing themselves inland, no earnest walkers on the winding tracks. And within three weeks the autumn started rolling in the mists which changed the view with every swirl; Marsh End no longer like a sunny summer rental but more an eerie grange touched by the chill of ghostly fingers. Damp got into old Nelson's timbers and the floor below Sophia suddenly cracked in the night or creaked like a ship at sea. How soon before she could get out of this? It was no good waiting for university – with no word from her mother's agent, how long before she just took off for London and Eli, became a missing person?

The Kent seaside was shut down for the season but Lesley's advert at the Dungeness RSPB sanctuary brought more bird-watchers to Marsh End. They were a peculiar, quiet lot who gave Sophia the creeps even more – not speaking above whispers for fear of frightening their prey, yet human enough all right for Sophia to catch men staring at her over their bird books and women taking surreptitious looks under the table linen to judge the worth of the furniture. Everyone's got an eye for something. But she could handle that – like a stroppy waitress she'd ask the men, 'Sorry? Were you were looking at me?' What she couldn't handle was the fact that nothing she did outside of her room was ever private, there was always someone around to see or hear what she was up to. Marsh End was neither her home nor even a house to live in – it was a public place where she led a public life worse than the Queen's. At least the Queen could tell everyone to get stuffed! And the weather – would these people never stop going on about the bloody weather? She always told them the opposite of the forecast, but then there were all the questions about her school and her future. So she was studying oceanography and going to be an astronaut – that got some of them going, being so RSPB pernickety. *I'd like anything except growing into one of you!* she wanted to say – and did to one deaf woman. Eli said she couldn't believe it when she told her in an e-mail.

But still Sophia plotted to get away – even the *thought* of her plans helped – and she found an escape; everyone needs a way of escape. At weekends she simply got out of the place. She did her chores so Lesley couldn't have a go at her, and then she got out. Sometimes it would be with Jenny, Jenny was great company, but Sol was around more and more these days and Sophia always felt uneasy with him; she didn't want to be shaken out of her mood by some big brother comment – and he always did that, always made her feel a *girl*. What Sophia found she needed most of all was to be on her own, and she found just the place to be private and alone, away from everyone.

It was about a mile away from Marsh End, a place she came across by accident, cycling round the lanes. After a couple of visits it became the place she'd head for – although no one went anywhere on the marsh roads straight off, they followed the dyke banks and went in all directions to get nowhere. But this spot was worth keeping secret by such deviations because it really was private, a small sort of grotto under a stone arch where lovers would have met in old stories; a ruined tower standing alone, held together by climbing ivy – well away from the nearest road, across a field of sheep in the middle of a small wood. It could have been an old church or chapel, long since fallen down, its remains hidden now under overhanging branches, old walls reaching up into the leaves and arching over, with a space about two metres square at the bottom. Sophia called it Micheli Tower, and it was here that she would ditch her bike and unlock her five-year diary.

A secret place where someone goes
Inside her head.
No ears, no eyes, no reading
Of her look.
No chance that anybody knows
Who's here,
What tears she sheds, what scribbling
In her book,
Who she speaks to as her pen
Talks thoughts;
Whose spirit mind her writings link
To hers.
'I'm me, you're you,
You're me, I'm you—
Or sometimes would be
If my hopes were ink.'

In this place she went back years to junior school days as she made a sort of camp; a camp only being a camp if you occupy it. She and Eli had once made one on a day out to Epping Forest on the bus – left a personal item each to make the place theirs – but they never went back, so Eli lost a ribbon and Sophia lost a *Mizz* bracelet. But when she'd proved she could find Micheli Tower again she hid a piece of plastic sheeting for sitting on in the cracks between ancient stones. And she hid an old kitchen knife, and a throwaway lighter she'd found. She marked her territory with secret stones stepped out, and off the barbed wire fence she collected wool dry enough for fire lighting and wrapped it in the plastic sheet. She found a comfortable place to sit in any weather on a smooth stone under the arch, and another place to lie out in the corner of the field where she couldn't be seen. Last of all she took a tin of baked beans – but forgot the can opener.

This was where she could be alone, where she was the Sophia underneath, where she could mourn her father's death and cry if she wanted; where she could phone Eli with really private stuff; where she didn't have to be the cool teenager seeing off the dirty looks of old men or be polite to their whiskery wives; and where she didn't have to keep her opinions below a whisper in the kitchen. Here she could stand up, strip naked if she wanted and shout at the smug sky – and she did once, till she thought her father might be looking. Here she could sit and hug herself, cry at the memory of jokes and meals and walks and romps, the swimming, the cycling, the riding, the watching Spurs, the going to previews, the listening to band practice and the hearing of the soft blues jazz Toni played for himself. Here she could remember those ordinary things of life that she'd taken so much for granted – argued over, even – because she hadn't known that there wouldn't be a tomorrow when none of it would happen any more.

This was Micheli Tower. This was where the old Micheli life could be relived and where it could be mourned. And where she was shocked to screaming one day, when the mists had rolled in on her, and a voice suddenly burst through the fringe of tree.

'It's you! Hiya!' Then, 'Sorry, Cav! Didn't want to scare you.'

Scared? She was petrified, huddled round behind a tree. But, '"Cav"?' It was Sol Barton.

'Caviar and lettuce. My caviar girl!' He was high stepping through the thicket in his motor-cycling boots.

'I'm nobody's girl.' She clutched her diary behind her back as she came to face him off. 'Well, not yours.' Her voice was as thin as an angry scare. She thought about hitting him with the hidden tin of baked beans but she couldn't remember where she'd put it.

He came into her camp, smiled, and sat on her smooth stone. 'Didn't you hear my bike?' He pointed way back towards the road.

Sophia stooped and thrust her diary quickly into

her shoulder bag. 'Did you follow me?' She crossed her arms, the landowner.

'Me follow you? You sure that's not the other way around?' he asked. 'You're in the best private place this end of the marsh. The best ever place for secret things. My place. *You* could have followed *me* here, the last time I came.'

So he came here, too; he probably brought his girlfriends out here on the back of his Honda. That was the trouble with most secret places, someone's got them bagged.

He smiled up at her. 'You want to know why I come?'

'No thank you.'

'I'll show you anyway.' And as she squinted her eyes, a fraction off shutting them tight, his hand went for the pocket of his jeans; from which he pulled a shiny, midnight blue mouth organ, the same colour as the inside of her father's saxophone case. Settling, he put it to his mouth and ran a scale up and down to wet it, worked it into his lips and started playing the opening of *Mood Indigo*. 'People take the piss,' he said, breaking off, 'they hum me the right note when I go wrong as if I don't know what it ought to be; blokes at work, Jen and Mum, the old man when he was home; so I come out here. You never get stuff right the first time, and these old sheep don't mind the fluffs.'

For the first time since his scary arrival Sophia found breathing easier. 'My dad was a musician,' she told him.

Sol nodded in a way that said he knew already. Jenny must have told him – or he'd asked her. He played another phrase of the blues with his eyes closed. 'Now, I've shown you mine, so you show me yours.' But he said it with a soft tone that somehow wasn't dirty.

Sophia looked at him hard. He might be a musician like her father but she wasn't sure about going that far. You might practise an instrument privately but you played it out loud. Telling him her secret wouldn't be equal swaps. Her scribbling was only for her; and even if some of it turned out perfect there was no way she'd ever let anyone read it.

'I come here to think,' she said, 'that's all – away from people at the house.' She took a deep breath and gave him a bit more because she thought he might understand. 'I miss my dad, and I...talk to him, too, out here.' Which was the truth. She also talked to him through her pillow; but she couldn't write at home, her mother could come in on her at any time, that was the secret difference.

Sol got up. Sophia could see the thought go through his head of putting his arm round her in comfort. But he stood off, bowed his head and said,

'I can understand that.' He turned away, then back again, laughing, 'I'd like to talk to mine, but what I'd say to him would sure as hell frighten the sheep.'

Sophia laughed, too. 'Well,' she said, looking round at Micheli Tower, 'if this isn't shared with a third party, you and I could have a rota.'

'Or we could come together and I'll play while you write.'

Sophia had half nodded before she hooked on to what he had said. 'Who said I write?'

'Writing's talking, isn't it? To a piece of paper, with a pen.' He nodded at the Bic which was still stupidly in her hand. 'Playing's talking, too – through the mood of a song. You know what Charles Aznavour said – you know Charles Aznavour?'

'Old French singer.' Of course Sophia knew him; her mother had worked on the design for a London show he'd once written.

'He said the words of a song dress the wounds of the audience.'

'Yeah, I understand that.'

'So we understand each other.' Sol put the harmonica to his mouth again and played the opening chords of Judy Garland's 'The Man that Got Away'.

Sophia listened, watched his fluttering fingers, his closed eyes which would open on a phrase and look at her. He was good, he made beautiful mournful music; his playing had to be his consolation where poetry was hers.

'No, you were here first,' she said, 'I'll find some other place.'

'Why?'

She didn't need to think about it. 'Because I don't want to choose between talking to you and...anyone else.'

'Choose? You wouldn't "want to choose"? So you wouldn't mind both, then?' he asked, 'in their place?'

Sophia didn't answer that, she didn't feel ready to. Instead, she just went; she picked up her bike and pushed through the trees, determined to come back some other time to collect her things. And Sol didn't try to stop her but played on, as if all that really mattered to him was making his music. Which Sophia appreciated, being Toni Micheli's daughter. All the same, despite the way she'd avoided him at Jenny's, she couldn't help feeling a bit disappointed that he didn't call goodbye.

Bri Tingle, Leonard's seasick 'muscle', couldn't speak a word of French but he knew the Calais run for cheap fags. Once the school holidays were over and cross Channel traffic was lighter he started to make regular trips over for cigarettes – acting suspiciously in his small Ford to get himself stopped and searched but keeping just within the limits on what he brought in. In that way Customs got to know the inside of Tingle's car almost as well as they knew their own and they were happy at there being no sniff of drugs nor any hiding place for an illegal immigrant: Tingle might be known London muscle but he was simply after regular, cheap snout. And that was the idea – that there'd be nothing remarkable about him coming and going, so that when he came back with what Frank Leonard wanted he could whistle on through like the wind. If the main man chose that option.

The French end of the operation Leonard was seeing to himself. Through people with second homes in France – friends of people he could frighten – he recruited four local heavies who were tough enough to handle Frenchie Donoghue, and paid them to be on standby for the Lydd flying weekend, airstrip to be announced. Which meant, altogether, that the prison screw was on board, the pilot and plane were set, the safe house at Sandgate was ready, the French muscle was in place, and Bri Tingle was organised to bring home the proceeds. Very pleasing.

After Frenchie Donoghue was liberated.

This Saturday Leonard was swimming in his indoor pool at Middle Marsh Manor. Frank Leonard had two styles – a hard splashy crawl when he was wound up over something, and a drift round on his back when he was pleased with himself. At the moment he was on his back, with Bev Leonard swimming alongside him doing her only style, on her front.

'You've waited long enough, Frank,' she said. 'So have I – an' diamonds *are* a girl's best friend.'

'You think I'm doing all this for you?'

'No, but some of it, eh? You like to see me sparkling here an' there... You used to, when you'd half kill a man who looked at me too long. When you took me off the modelling so only you ever got to see me...' She swam round to his floating feet and up over on top of him. 'I gave the best years of my looks to you...' She tried to kiss him.

'Watch it! You wanna drown me?'

'Only in my love, Frank.'

'Leave it out! Love? You greedy mare!' He suddenly grabbed her head and pushed her under, held her down there clamped between his thighs till her thrashing became frantic. And by the time she pulled herself out of the pool coughing her throat raw and snorting water down her nose, he was dry and getting into his clothes.

'I don't do nothing for *love*! Them diamonds is my pension, an' don't you forget it!'

It took all the courage Sophia could summon to go

back to Micheli Tower that Saturday evening. The marsh mist hovered over the dykes, mud sucked in the waterways, creatures scuttled into holes and soft old sheep looked like devil goats coming out of the dusk. Above the rubbery swish of her tyres Sophia could hear everything; but her bike lights could only show her the way ahead as far as the next patch of shifting mist. More than once she wobbled in nothingness and nearly ran off the road.

Then, Mother Mary! What was that? There was a sound somewhere behind her, a metallic sound, a sort of rattle, rattle, rattle. It came from a way back but it was getting closer and closer and closer. Her first instinct was to put on speed, to get away from it – but she couldn't with all the twists and the veils of grey, she was held back by her own blindness. And on it came behind, rattle, rattle, rattle – like the clanking of the gibbet chains where they used to hang marsh smugglers. But, weirdly, it was getting no nearer – the eerie sound seemed to be keeping pace with her, staying just behind her, just behind her all the time – uncanny and frightening, and as she passed Middle Marsh Manor heading for the Micheli Tower turn off she was ready to shout 'Help!' into the gate grille, or throw her bike into the verge and lie flat in the grass till the rattle had gone on past.

Rattle, rattle, rattle… But she was past the gate

grille now, it had come too suddenly in the mist and there was nothing else to do but throw herself into the verge – because she couldn't go on with this behind her. Except, when she looked down, the verge had narrowed to solid brick wall and there was nothing for it but to go on a bit further. Rattle, rattle, rattle. She was in a panic now, but suddenly there was a stretch of clear road ahead so she pushed her leading leg into a spurt – and ran floundering into a surprise swirl of head-high mist. Unable to stop, she lost her balance and crashed off the road into a scrap of hedge, only just saving herself from scraping down a bank into murky marsh water.

Rattle, rattle, rattle – stop. And now a figure was hovering above her like some ghoul.

'You all right, girl?' It was Fred Kiff, astride his bike with his cart of tools behind. That had been the rattle, rattle, rattle. 'Had you for being better balanced.'

Sophia pulled herself up, bridled at him. 'Well if I'm unbalanced it's because of your spooky rattling.' She picked up her bike and spun her wheels; no damage done.

The old man laughed. 'Spooky? Me? That red light o' your'n was waving about in front like a Jack o' Lantern – I thought the marsh spirits was abroad...' He had taken off his creased brown cap and was scratching his head.

Sophia shivered: it was really scary out here when the mists were up and the light was gone. She turned her bike around to go home.

'Well might you shiver, girl. You've come to the right place for ghosts. Smugglers in chains on the gibbet an' revenue men drowned in the dykes, skeletons buried in old collapsed tunnels where they came and went with contraband...'

Sophia set her handlebars straight for pushing off. She didn't want to hear anything else gruesome until it was bright daylight in the safety of Marsh End.

'Goo'night to you, then.' And without another word Fred Kiff was off wherever he was going, rattle, rattle, rattling on.

She forgot Micheli Tower. She half rode, half scooted back along the way she'd come. But she was wrong if she thought her journey with following noises was over – because something else came up behind her, although the sound of the motor bike didn't plague her for long before it overtook. It was going somewhere else, as fast as the mist and the twist allowed, but it hadn't gone the length of its own headlamps before it squealed rubber in an emergency stop. It was the Honda.

'Cav!' said Sol as his lifted his crash helmet, knight in armour style, shaking out his long hair. 'Not been to our place, have you?'

Our place! 'No! You have it. I said.' She wasn't going to tell him that's where she'd been heading.

'You don't believe in sharing, then?'

His voice was deeper than any of the boys at Sophia's old school, or Jon Elite's at Club Seventeen. Jenny said he was nineteen, old enough to vote, working, a man. And she was pleased that he hadn't caught her in her naff school uniform.

'Listen, it's easy, sharing—' he was going on, '—if you get there and see the bike or hear the harmonica, then I'm there. If I get there and hear you talking to yourself, then you're there. I'll leave you in peace and you leave me. How about that?'

Sophia wanted to be safe indoors now, she wasn't into arguing over a stupid secret place! 'Whatever…'

'"Whatever"? I take that as a yes? That's a deal, then?' And he took his hand out of his gauntlet to shake on it. Reluctantly she offered hers, and found his palm warm on the cold night, and smooth, like her father's; and he held on. 'I was hoping to bump into you sometime, don't fancy using Jenny for passing messages…'

'Oh, I'm sure she'd remember them OK.' Jenny was Sophia's friend; she wasn't going to talk about Jenny except in nice ways, not even to Sol.

'Yeah, but this is an invitation, and I might be able to get one for her, but I've already got the two…'

'To what?' Straddling her bike, him holding her hand, it was very hard for Sophia to look cool and unapproachable.

'Firm's annual disco. Digital South. Tickets sell like—'

'Hot digits?' She took her hand away.

'Along at Hythe, Friday the fourteenth of October. Fancy coming?'

'With you?'

'Who else?'

'I dunno.' It was a complicated issue, it needed thinking through – her being a friend of his sister, Jen not sure of a ticket even, and other things – Sophia wasn't up for a quick yes or a quick no.

'Have you got to ask your mother?' Then Sol added gently, 'Or your father?'

And that decided Sophia; Sol Barton seemed to understand her.

'I've got to *tell* my mother,' Sophia said, 'nearer the time. But yes, I'll come if I can. Thank you.' Now she needed to get away, to think about all this, to get indoors before it all turned out to be marsh mist. She hitched herself up on to her saddle and swore at having to wobble as she went. 'See you!'

He put on his helmet and kick-started the Honda. 'See you, Cav!'

He went his way and she went hers, heading for

Marsh End where she would creep as quietly as she could up the back stairs and to her room. The last thing she wanted was to meet a guest and have to be normal; they might read the slight smile on her face. Her mother definitely would.

Would you like him? Would you let me go?
Is he your sort of man?
Would you trust him with your daughter riding at
his back,
Roaring down the road with a wind-taken shout
For lovers' talk?
Is he your sort of man?
Breathing out a tune with a kissing mouth,
Vibrato tongue, wing-fingered, soft chords of love—
Lips busy, but eyes that look their love at me.
Is he your sort of man—
And would you let me go?

In the mist before her Sophia saw her father looking at her, that shrewd Italian expression on his face; now he would either shake his head and waggle his fingers in a no; or pick up his sax to nod a yes into the opening bars of *Mood Indigo*. But as she rode he vanished, and she still wasn't sure which way his decision would go.

CHAPTER SEVEN

Frenchie Donoghue's move was all of the surprise he'd been told it would be. And more. The words he'd been waiting for came at him when he least expected them. Wednesdays were local court days, when all the transport was taken up getting remand prisoners in front of magistrates: there was nothing left over for routine transfers between prisons – those were usually weekend jobs. But at six o'clock on Wednesday the twelfth came the clank at Frenchie's cell door, and the shout, 'Get your gear, Donoghue, you're on the move.'

And, *real* surprise – it was the Wing Manager who'd given him the knock and not the landing screw. He'd brought a tray of breakfast with him because 'transfers' didn't mix with the other cons once they were on their way out; the prisons they were going to didn't want drugs or tobacco brought into their regimes from other places. But if Donoghue had been given anything and stashed it in his cell there was no chance for him to get at it. While he ate his breakfast and drank the 'diesel', which was over-sweetened tea, two other screws turned the place inside out for any sight of little plastic packets. Donoghue watched them with his nose pulled into a sneer – or it might have been the sickly tea – because he'd kept himself clean for five years to get a transfer down to category B so no way was he going to blow it by messing with drugs. There was just his personal stereo, his magazines, a pin-up photograph of a girl and his phone cards – everything else belonged to Her Majesty.

'You've got a good day for it, Donoghue!' One of the screws used his usual tactic for winding up the cons – talking about the weather. 'Inside' is one place where the weather is of no concern whatever – the walls are thick enough, the windows small enough and the sky in such short supply that the state of the weather doesn't come into things. Screws talking about the beautiful weekend forecast is sand in prisoners' eyes.

But even in Wyck Hill Prison out at the estuary, the weather that Wednesday morning was starting to be felt. It had been an October night of growing high winds coming in off the North Sea, and now it was rattling bars, whistling in triple locks, and finding the gaps in screws' weatherproofs – a rage of wet at

Beaufort Scale Nine, draped black over the south of England. Heathrow air traffic was diverted to Birmingham and the Dartford road bridge was closed as it twisted over the river in a giant cats' cradle.

'Better than too hot,' Donoghue chewed at the screw. 'Don' fancy a sweat box in the hot.' Sweat boxes were the old prison transports driven by Securicor, Group Four or VanGuard – armoured vehicles partitioned into individual locked-door cells, some for one, some for four, some for eight, and the big 'buses' for twelve or more. But Donoghue had been in prison some time – these days they came air conditioned, as he was told.

The searching screws looked at one another and shook their heads; the cell was clean, and no surprise to them because Donoghue had worked for his downgrade harder than a head boy at a Catholic school.

'Right, we'll get you down to Reception an' let the lads have a look up your arse.'

The other screws laughed. 'Best part of their day. Let's hope they've had their breakfast!'

With all the other cells in the section banged-up, Frenchie Donoghue carried his pillowcase of belongings along the landing to the stairs. He shouted a loud, 'See you, boys! Frenchie's off!' and got a few shouts and a banging of mugs on bed legs as respectful goodbyes. He was taken off the wing and down to Reception where a thorough body search was carried out – but there was no sadistic pleasure taken and no joy in Donoghue's going because he'd been a model prisoner. There were other violent cases they'd have been better pleased to see 'shanghaied'.

'Come on! Come on!' The Wing Manager hurried everyone up, 'I got a busy day.'

'You don't have to stay, guv,' Reception told him. 'We'll see him off.'

'*I'll* see him off, and to time!' they were told. 'This is one I want away prompt.' Then he added, 'Garside's difficult on market day…'

And he watched and pushed things along, even carrying Donoghue's papers out to the driver of the transport; so that in under half an hour from the first word the prisoner was inside the wind-rocked VanGuard prison bus having a rub-down search.

'We've done all that.' The Wing Manager took another look at his watch. But these private company guards had their own responsibility for a prisoner and they wouldn't take any prison screw's word that someone was clean.

Donoghue was put into a cell and its sliding door floor bolted – in a bus for eight but Frenchie their only passenger, with a driver up front in the cab and a guard in the back. Frenchie sat in the tight seat and looked out of the darkened window where there was nothing to see for a while but rain-lashed Wyck Hill wall. He banged on the door before they started.

'What?'

'You got the air con on?'

'Not hot enough for that. You'll be in Garside, under the hour.'

'It's boiling!' Donoghue complained.

'It ain't! It's bleedin' wet an' bleedin' windy an' bleedin' cold.'

'Well I'm *hot*.' Donoghue wiped the sweat from his neck.

'An' I'm *cold*, so shut it!' And the guard gave the word for the bus to go.

Back in his office the Wing Manager who'd woken the prisoner, taken him his breakfast and personally seen him out through Reception, checked his watch one more time and picked up his phone. 'Job done, seven ten,' he said. 'Bus on the move, seven forty.' He didn't wait for any reply; calls over twenty seconds started getting logged. But from his desk he sat and watched the CCTV monitor show the main gate of Wyck Hill open and Frenchie Donoghue start on a journey he didn't know he was taking.

The VanGuard bus turned left out of the prison and headed for the A133 towards Colchester and the A12. In the driving rain everything was moving slowly, only windscreen wipers going at full speed. As the bus turned on to the dual carriageway the wind hit its higher sides and the driver had to start holding hard on to his wheel. But he didn't have to keep to anyone else's speed. With a category A transfer or a terrorist going to court there would have been an outriding escort, but with a downgrade to category B the only other vehicle near them on the road was one following. It was a black car staying behind the bus, someone keeping tabs on Frenchie Donoghue.

Lesley had a surprise that morning, too. As well as friends and family, people from her past had phoned her all the time since the move – always with cheerful talk about what was going on, dishing the gossip, how *was* she? And didn't everyone miss her? But people in the theatre world are busy, their lives change swiftly; and the calls were much less frequent now. So this Wednesday morning in October when show biz was either working or asleep, the phone call came as a surprise.

She was busy, three of the four double bedrooms were full and there were some hearty breakfasts to clear away. Right now it was atrocious outside, a buffeting wind pounding the house like a high sea and the rain coming off the marsh like grapeshot. It was hard to see across the road through such heavy weather – and there'd definitely been no bike ride for

Sophia, she'd gone to school in Jenny's mother's car instead of cycling to the bus at Dymchurch. Paying guests were sitting about in the sitting room and the conservatory reading their newspapers, maps and bird books, giving off an 'Oooh!' or an 'Aaah!' or a 'Look at that!' whenever a gust shook the glass in the window frames. The dishwasher was busy, the pans were soaking in the deep sink, the fridge door was open as the sideboard was cleared – and the telephone rang. But this was probably a booking, someone looking forward to decent weather, so Lesley dropped everything to answer it.

'Marsh End.' She had her big diary and a pen handy for taking the booking.

'Les Micheli?' asked a woman's smoky voice.

'Yes.'

'It's Bee du Pont.'

'Oh, hello. How did *you* get this number?' Hardly a warm welcome.

'A friend of a friend, Les. Through your agent.' Bee broke off for a crackly cough – or it could have been the telephone line in the storm. 'Listen, you're joking, aren't you?'

'Joking?'

'Burying yourself in the country?'

'I don't think so.'

A listening guest must have heard the chill in

Lesley's voice. He moved away, got up and felt a radiator.

'Word was you'd got it out of your system. Listen, I want you for a show.'

Lesley stared at the ceiling. 'Sorry, Bee, I'm not available. I retired – didn't your friend of a friend tell you?'

'But this'll tempt you back, love. A new *Arms and the Man*, all star cast – Bobbie Sexton *asked* for you, your agent's up for it – opens at the London Haymarket December sixteenth—'

'I *told* you—'

The line did go dead now, just for a second.

'Are you there?' Bee coughed.

'There's a storm blowing down here...'

'Ah, "the roads are up and the lines are down!" Same here. Listen, Les, this is Arts Council and European money; duplicate sets, one for London, one on tour in all the EU capitals with international casts. You're paid twice! The money is *mega,* love, and the kudos *supreme*. This is going to be so *big*! They'll want you designing all over Europe. I can give you ten days before I go elsewhere...'

Lesley sighed. 'Bee – there *is* something wrong with this line because you're not hearing me. I've had this conversation with a lot of other people before you and I'm sorry that you're the last to know. I've retired from the theatre and I'm doing something else, OK?'

'Cooking breakfasts and dusting under beds, I hear.'

'Then you hear correct, Bee, you hear correct.' And Lesley put down the phone with a crack to rival a *Revenge* beam settling in the night. Avoiding the eye of any of her marooned guests she went about her business; but anyone who knew her would have noticed an even more determined swing to her movements.

'Been a few heads of beautiful hair in that spare crash helmet,' Jenny told Sophia, pushing along a blustering corridor at lesson change as the storm outside forced everyone through one glass walkway. 'Yours won't be the first, Sofe.'

Sophia didn't have to answer as she led on through the ruck. Was Jenny upset? She'd never seemed the sort to take offence – but she was getting too good a mate for there to be any confusion about their friendship. Sol had got the extra ticket and Jenny was coming to the disco, which would definitely be a help when Sophia told her mother, and Sol was going to take one, then the other, on his pillion from the Bartons' house. Sophia saw it as a threesome, no way did she want to cut Jenny out – but was Jenny jealous that Sophia would be giving her attention to her brother all evening?

'They've all been pretty, I give him that. No old dogs up to now.'

'Cheers!' said Sophia. '"Up to now"? Is that with me counted in or counted out?'

'In, of course. You're a raver. But I'm worried about—'

'My extreme beauty sending him ape?'

Jenny stopped and pulled Sophia back, as if this had to be said standing still. '—I'm worried about him. He's getting too serious – and he's a *man*, he goes to *work*. He's mucked around with girls and always played his jazzy music, but since he walked in on you he's changed his tune, it's getting real heavy these days…'

'Heavy?' What wind was blowing, what rain pelting, what storm crashing? All Sophia could hear right now was what Jenny was saying. 'How, heavy?'

'I told you, his music.' Jenny led on again. 'They're all love songs; and where he goes off to practise I don't know, but he's got them perfect. He's forever looking out the window and playing them for you, Sofe, I know – and at his age it's *serious*.'

Sophia tried for a second to look unfazed.

'Or it could just be—' Jenny went on over her

shoulder '—that he's bought a new song book.'

'Yeah,' said Sophia, 'that's probably it.' And she skipped on after her friend.

If the bird-watchers at Marsh End were fair weather sorts that Wednesday, huddling indoors while the storm blew round the house, another was out and about as she always was. This was the woman who had surprised Sophia coming up out of the barley near Middle Marsh Manor, the bird-watcher who could have made Fred Kiff wrong about skylarks. Today her cycling cape was throwing itself round her neck and slapping at her legs in frenzied whips as she stood in the porch of St James', the disused church at Fallow Broad. She could have sheltered inside because the door was kept unlocked, but her eyes were for the outside. Even the birds were grounded but the woman's eyes weren't in the air – they were staring at the road; and they hardly blinked in the beating rain until along the narrow road came a Mercedes, headlamps on in the wet. The car went splashing past as the woman hurried from the church porch, ran to her van in the lay-by, and followed it along the marsh road towards Sandgate.

The Nelson at Sandgate was battened down on the beach side. Smaller shingle was being whipped up and flung stinging at the doors and windows as the storm crashed in off the sea, rearranging the beach in new mounds of tossed stone. In these conditions, Frank Leonard used the front door. Inside, round a log fire, a couple of Sandgate pensioners were ordering their lunch from the menu board while a couple of spry locals drank theirs. Terry Ford was taking the orders ready for the girl out at the back to put them in the microwave. He just hesitated a second in his scribbling when Frank Leonard walked in.

The pensioners smiled at the man, but the locals hardly swivelled as he ran his hands through his wet hair and down his soaking face.

'Wet enough for you?' an old man asked.

'Could say that,' Leonard replied, turning his face away and his collar up.

Terry Ford stood waiting for the word.

'It's cod an' chips for one. As ordered,' Leonard said.

'Right you are, sir.'

'Give it an hour or so.'

'No prob.'

Leonard went past the bar and on through the door marked Toilets towards the back and the stairs to check the accommodation. On the way he passed the girl from before who was busy in the kitchen. She looked at him and drew in a big breath, flattened her stomach, pushed herself out at the top and smiled.

Leonard stopped on the stair. 'That's the ticket!' he said. 'You keep my guest sweet for a coupla days!'

But right now Frenchie Donoghue wasn't sweet and wasn't well. He was suffering in a big way in his claustrophobic VanGuard cell. His banging and moaning and the sudden sound of him retching brought the vehicle guard sliding to his spyhole. The prisoner looked woozy, as if he couldn't breathe, his skin seemed ice-cold blue, but sweat was pouring off him like a melting glacier.

'Christ! He's having a heart attack!'

The guard had three options, because the company wouldn't stand for a death in transit. The policy was: they headed for the nearest prison with a medical wing, like pulling back to Wyck Hill; they diverted to a police station with a doctor on tap – or they went for the Accident and Emergency department of the nearest hospital. And this attack looked bad enough for that. He unlocked Donoghue's door to get him more air and shot a look out through the smoked glass window. They were on the A road heading west, nowhere near Garside or any other prison.

He shouted through the intercom at his driver. 'Queen Mary's, Totham – hospital, quick! This bloke's going!'

Donoghue was moaning and swearing and

starting to bring up his breakfast.

'He's gonna choke on his own vomit!' The guard found the emergency water and dabbed the prisoner with it, trying to give him sips with a plastic cup. But more was coming up than going down and the prisoner's head was lolling and banging against the side of the bus. He cracked one side then the other as it took a sudden swerve to the nearside lane, the guard hanging on before grabbing for his radio to alert the Essex Police. Policy again, procedure: if a prisoner had to be taken to hospital in transit they needed uniformed back-up.

The violent weather banged in across the local playing fields as the vehicle rammed its way through to the Totham turn-off at Hardy's Corner.

'Get a move on, Del – we don't want to give 'em a "Dead on Arrival". If he's going to croak let 'im do it in there!'

His driver didn't answer, he was too busy with the tricky road, going through a red light to take a right down the hospital approach and past the helicopter pad into the ambulance entrance at Queen Mary's. The bus stopped with a sudden crack of Donoghue's head on the partition as the driver braked hard and backed in fast as if this were the Old Bailey yard. He jumped out of his cab to run in to A and E for assistance.

Uniforms soon get people jumping, and in no time two orderlies and a nurse were at the bus with a trolley. It took some manoeuvring to get the unconscious man out of his cell and out through the back door, but as swift as a Porsche at a pit stop he was inside a cubicle and being hitched to a heart machine.

A young female doctor came running, so did two uniformed policemen.

'You was quick!' the guard told them.

'Yeah, we was handy. Who's this?'

'Donoghue, on transfer Wyck Hill to Garside. Been and thrown a heart attack at us!'

'Possibly,' said the doctor, working at pulse and blood pressure. 'Nurse, get me an airway.' The nurse hurried out through the curtains.

'So he's ours now.' The policeman pulled a face at the guard. 'Out of your bus an' in our patch.'

'Is he?'

'Why, d'you want him back, like this?'

The guard shook his head.

'You get back to your vehicle an' make your report to both prisons, we'll sit on chummy.'

The guard turned to the doctor. 'He is alive, isn't he? I can tell 'em he's alive up to now?'

The doctor nodded. With a look of relief the guard went – his footsteps just out of earshot on the polished lino when suddenly a big hand was clamped hard over the doctor's mouth.

'Steady, girl! Steady!' It was one of the policemen. She struggled against his powerful arm and mumbled into his hand, but she could do nothing to stop the other policeman from ripping Donoghue from the heart machine and starting to push the trolley out of the cubicle. There were people about but no one stopped him, policemen in uniform are always doing lawful things. At speed he took a left along the corridor towards the outpatients' department.

'Sorry, doll,' the first policeman said into the doctor's ear. 'Don't want you panicking, but this is political, MI6, terrorist stuff. Them transit guys don't know it but he ain't had no heart attack, he's stoned on drugs.' He lifted his hand from her mouth as the nurse arrived with the plastic airway.

'That's still assault!' the doctor blistered at him. 'I'm not "doll" and I don't panic!' She was shaking with shock and indignation, so much so that the nurse didn't even ask where the patient was. 'Heart attack or drugs – and I was about to tell you this was no heart attack, his pupils are like pinpricks – he is in *my* hospital and he is *my* patient! What's your number?'

The policeman shrugged his shoulders, but his face said that he was still in the right. He pointed to his shoulder. 'PC Spring,' he said.

'Where are you taking him?'

'Back in the transport,' he said. 'They made a balls-up of it, coming in here. Don't worry, it'll go in the report.' He opened the curtains, looked left and right and suddenly went, pulling them closed behind him. But instead of heading for the ambulance entrance he slipped along the corridor in the direction the trolley had taken, lost in the traffic of people.

The doctor and the nurse groped with the closed curtains and came running out towards the VanGuard bus at the front – failing to see two policemen wheel a shrouded body from fifty yards further down the building and load it into the back of a black windowless van.

While the bewildered transport guards were being faced with two angry medics an Essex police car arrived in a swathe of spray, all capes and wet radios. The black van passed them and drove away in the storm as they turned in. 'PC Spring' turned to his companion, who was driving. 'Done that all right,' he said. 'Didn't even 'ave to tangle with the Bill. Where's the next car switch?'

'Crow Green, Bri,' said the other. 'Then this gets dumped up Harwich, near the docks.'

'Nice one,' said Bri Tingle. 'An' I get a fish dinner down the Kent coast.'

CHAPTER EIGHT

Fred Kiff came to Marsh End as quickly as he could, around ten o'clock. Today he wasn't on his bike trundling his tools behind him, but in a battered old car, nosing through wicked weather that seemed set to go on for ever.

'Sorry, Missus, everyone's in trouble today. When the rain comes at you sideways it gets into more holes than a flock o' sheeps' backsides. If you'll pardon the met-aphor.'

But Lesley was quite used to vulgar sayings, working in the theatre; and it *was* an aperture that had forced her to call him. There were cracks in the old upright feather-boarding of the back door, but the main problem was the rain driving underneath in a long triangle of blown wet where the *Revenge* door frame pitched its foot at an angle. She'd been stuffing it with rags all morning but they were sodden in no time.

In his long, oiled mac and a lifeboatman's sou'wester Fred Kiff studied the problem from outside and in, excusing himself for puddling on the stone floor.

'I'll nail a patch of tarpaulin on,' he told Lesley, 'you've got a roll in your barn. Then we'll fashion a new foot to your door when the sun's a'shining.' And he set to with a razor-sharp fisherman's knife and a mouthful of clout nails, talking all the while round the spikes, asking how business was and all that. But while some nosy people give offence, Fred Kiff didn't because he was so open about it. 'Oh, I like knowing all the ins an' outs,' he told Lesley when he'd heard about the rooms and the en-suites, what was occupied and what was not. 'Ears an' eyes of the marsh, I am.'

He hadn't finished before Jenny's mother, sent home from working in a flooded office, kindly dropped Sophia off from school. Any students who could be collected were being allowed home in the storm, the south of England now in a Weather Alert. The two women had met only briefly earlier when Mrs Barton had collected Sophia, so Lesley invited Jenny and her mother in for a cup of tea, through in the dining room away from Fred Kiff's hammering.

Even in the quick run from the car Sophia was soaked, and her blazer gave off that pungent smell of burnt cork. But there was no way she could take herself off to change because it was suddenly too compelling watching these two women size each other up: the two mothers she'd compared. She'd told each about the other, but they hadn't met properly. Now here they were, doing what Sophia had done, comparing their situations. Both were women on their own, each had a daughter who shared their loss, and both played life at its own hard game. It was just that Mrs Barton was playing at home, Sophia thought, and her mother away. They talked about nothing as important as the loss of their husbands, but Sophia knew what the subtext was beneath the eyeing of hands, the checking of shoes and the stares at each other as they went on about how deserted the marsh got in the winter and the atrocious weather that was banging the doors. They were birds of a very different feather, Sophia decided: her mother shorter, younger looking, rounder in the face; Jenny's sitting taller, more sombre, somehow in her attitude suffering more for her loss – although her husband wasn't even dead. Was that the difference between them then? One had been left for someone else, the other had just been left? And to be honest the first had to be harder to take, being walked out on, a slap in the face as well as a slammed door. It had certainly brought more grieving.

The two girls sat and drank Cokes in silence until Jenny was suddenly pitched into the conversation by a burp that needed covering – all at once wanting to know how Marsh End got judged for Tourist Board diamonds. Would that tarpaulin on the back door bring them down? 'Who deee-cides?' she asked, round another bout of wind. Sophia had to hide behind her hands – she couldn't believe this!

Mrs Barton came to Jenny's rescue, a diversion with a nod back at the kitchen. 'I see you've got Mr Kiff in.'

'More out than in,' Lesley said, 'judging by the draught!'

'What a weird little man. Pots of money, they say, but where does it come from? He'll charge you peanuts for that. Odd jobbing and fishing and a field of sheep? You should see his boat...'

'I have;' said Sophia, 'in the dyke. It's like a little punt.'

'Oh, not that one,' Jenny said, with hiccups now. 'He's got one in Rye Harbour, very posh. Like a dustman driving a Rolls-Royce...'

'Really?' Lesley looked back towards the kitchen where the hammering had stopped – and on cue in came Fred Kiff to stand dripping in the doorway.

'That's done it, Missus, for now.' His weathered face was like a *Revenge* timber off the man o' war itself. 'Old door's sat-urated, needs caulking to stop the wet stuff comin' in. Or a new door.'

Lesley pointed to the telephone table in the hallway.

'Sofe – get the Bank of England.' Which was the make-up bag of loose cash Lesley used for this and that.

Sophia got there but Fred Kiff wouldn't take anything. 'Not done yet. You pay me for the full job come good weather.'

'It's up to you, but I'm very, very grateful…'

The odd-job man was turning to go when a phone went, the chirpy ring of a mobile that had everyone checking their bags and pockets; but to general surprise it was Fred Kiff who had the call. He dug deep in his waterproof and brought out a little gem of a new Samsung.

'Hello? Yeah. Righto.' He switched off, put the phone away. 'There's trouble all over the marsh,' he said. 'I'll bid you good day.' And with a move a bit faster than his usual shuffle he went for the repaired back door, followed once more by Lesley's gratitude.

But all this happened while Sophia was somewhere else. On the memo pad by the telephone was a name from the past, a name she'd worked to see, one that would have had her mother flapping her arms for quiet had a call from her ever come back in London – Bee du Pont of Westwood Productions: the queen of theatre, the maker and breaker of names. Had her mother's agent done the trick, had *she* phoned, the great Bee? Was there a chance her mother was being made an offer she couldn't refuse?

It was someone else's name, though, that suddenly shook the room for Sophia like a violent gust and brought her thumping back to present company.

'So you're going to the disco with Solomon?' Jenny's mother was saying.

'Eh? Solomon?' asked Sophia, who knew that she was going redder than ten Jennys.

'*Solomon?*' asked Lesley. 'Who's he?'

'My Solomon,' said Mrs Barton, looking from one to another as she got up. 'Sol. I'm sure he said you were going.' Her voice took on a teasing edge that didn't suit her. 'I know he'll be very upset if you're not...'

'I'm going with Jenny too,' Sophia just about got out. 'Jen's coming.' She had meant to tell her mother about her friend's brother, it had been at the top of her agenda for three weeks but somehow it had never happened – there were always people about, even knocking on the door of the kitchen in the evening for this and that – the chance just hadn't arisen. In the end, happy in her mind about what her father would have said, she'd got to the point where going with Jenny seemed enough for her mother to know.

'Yeah, I'm going. Sophia first, then me. On his pillion,' Jenny said – and made a revving noise.

'Oh, really?' Sophia asked, 'not on the bus?' – but knowing that she hadn't fooled her mother one bit.

'We hadn't discussed any of that,' Lesley said tartly

to Mrs Barton, 'if you'd tell Solomon.' It was like the way she'd stop someone short who was trying to get away with a cut in design or material. 'How old is your son?'

'Oh, he's nearly twenty,' Jenny's mother replied – to Sophia's despair not 'reading' this at all. 'The man of the house!'

Sophia could see the almost three years' difference in their ages registering in her mother's mind; registering and being saved for the row to come.

'Solomon knows his way about.'

Oh, God! thought Sophia. Shut up, woman! Because while Mrs Barton was saying it, her mother was staring not at Sophia's face but at her body. And it wasn't five minutes after Jenny and her mother went that Vesuvius blew. For this, Sophia was taken to the greater privacy of the wet-floored kitchen, but with one pair of guests now at the dining room bookcase and another pair in their bedroom on the first floor, it had to be in hoarse whispers.

'So who's this *man*? You haven't told me you're going with a *man*!'

'He's not a man, he's a boy. He'd have only just left third year sixth if he hadn't left early.'

'He's male.'

'Yeah – he's definitely the other sex, although I can't say I've checked!'

Not the bat of an eye interrupted Lesley's angry stare. 'With a motorbike!'

Sophia made a face as if this were a bedtime story with a monster just come on the scene. 'Yes, a big, big motorbike! You seen the little boys my age?'

Lesley opened and slammed shut a drawer for no reason and shouted an angry whisper. 'Do you think I want to *contemplate* another road accident in this family? Another…tragedy?'

Sophia hissed back: 'You've already dragged me down here, that's tragedy enough, you're not dragging me into the Middle Ages!' She stood with her back to the door of the *Revenge* kitchen, the repair tarpaulin sucking and blowing at her feet, her black boots squelching with rain that had run off her legs, still in her soaked clothes and draggled hair. She felt like a tart off some wet street corner as she bent forward from the waist in a thrust of anger at this stupid woman who thought they could live life away from it all with no danger in anything they did, wrapped in country wool.

'What are you scared of, him or his motorbike?' she shouted at her mother – really shouted, took on the storm. 'What's getting you out of your pram – his pillion or his prick?'

Even as she said it Sophia couldn't believe that she had. But her mother's face told her she had all right –

she'd blasted her with a crack of foul mouth.

'How dare you! You little fool!' Lesley screeched in a thin, hoarse thread that had her throat rasping. She lifted a hand, and dropped it. 'I'm scared of *both* – every mother's scared of both for her daughter – and I'm scared of you, too!'

'*Me?*'

Lesley's face turned acrid. '*You!* You've lost your...boundaries. Why keep him secret? Eh?'

Sophia stared at this face she didn't know, this woman she *despised* right now. And God knew what possessed her, but she let her have it. 'Girls only tell their mothers things if – if – if they *love* them!' She shouted it at Lesley loud enough to tell not just the house but their end of the marsh. And she pushed at the kitchen door and slammed outside to run against the whipping, solid rain to the barn. Then, because she thought her mother might follow her out, she went on past it along the flooding marsh road towards her secret place.

Frenchie Donoghue was coming round, the here and now seeping in through the porous rock of his headache. The third car he'd been crammed into was making slow progress down the river that was the M20 towards Ashford and the Channel Tunnel. He stared muzzily out of the window, his head lolling from side to side, but there was nothing to see in the storm – and he wasn't up to asking any questions. Bri Tingle who was sitting on one side of him with one of his doormen on the other, told him what was going on.

'You're the guest of someone you done a job with,' Tingle shouted against the whine of the wind and the pelt of the rain. 'He reckons you know where something is that he wants…'

Donoghue groaned.

'We've sprung you, son – now we're gonna bounce you round France till you take us to where them diamonds is hid. You receiving me?'

Donoghue groaned again.

'But first off we're going down the coast an' you're laying low for a coupla days, let the fresh sea air get prison out your lungs.'

Donoghue's answer was a violent spasm of sickness, all over Tingle's man, for which he got such a fist in the face that he couldn't get his mouth round the question of whose guest he was. Not that he needed to ask.

Bri Tingle laughed. 'Dirty bastard,' he said, 'that weren't in the script!'

On they drove along the forsaken roads. But what they didn't know as they stopped up a slip road for blue lights to flash past on the motorway, was that Frank Leonard's plans had been blown away in the storm. The hard bit had gone OK, but the easy bit was going badly wrong. Terry Ford from the Sandgate pub told Leonard he was gutted when he telephoned him at the Dome Club in Brighton – where Leonard was with his wife in the members' lounge, setting up his alibi well away from the action.

'I've clocked it three times – this camper van down the road, and no one's camping around in this weather. Every bird on the marsh has got its head up its arse but this woman's poncing around with binoculars focused on the Nelson. It ain't birds she's interested in, it's my pub.'

'What you saying? Someone's sitting on you – got wind of our plans for Donoghue?' Leonard's voice slid down to a deadly growl. 'You saying someone's grassed us up...?' Leonard's expression said that Terry Ford was very lucky they weren't face to face. 'You telling me to abort?'

'No, Frank. Hold off, that's all. It's been on the news an' the police on telly look lively as ants on flying day. Hole him up somewhere while I get this camper sussed...'

Leonard slammed down the phone on Terry Ford and swore. 'That bastard screw!' he hissed at Bev. 'He's playing a double game with someone!'

But Bev's face wasn't showing sympathy, it was showing concern. 'Why don't you abort, Frankie?'

she asked. 'We've been all right with what we've had. Let 'em find Donoghue, take him back inside...' She stroked Leonard's knee: she wasn't so svelte any more, but she was still a beautiful woman. 'You an' me, like the old days when we moved down here – we've got enough with everything else you've got going. Forget diamonds. Let's have the old dream team back again, eh, Frankie and Bevvy?'

'Dream team? Nightmares, more like!' Leonard turned his back on her and keyed in another number.

The mobile rang in Bri Tingle's pocket. 'Yeah?'

'Where are you?'

'A2070 – just past Warehouse.'

'Warehorn, you prat! Listen, forget the pub, it's being sat on. Stall a bit, I'll get back to you with a hide-out an' meet you there. Gotta be quick or they'll bug this. You got a map?'

'Somewhere.' Tingle leant over and started turning out the glove compartment.

Frenchie Donoghue, who was sitting up now and getting some colour in his face where he'd been hit, turned to his minder. 'You got problems?' he asked.

'You ain't one of 'em!' Tingle told him. 'Right,' he said into the phone. 'Got the map. I'll wait for your call.'

And as the kidnap car pushed on through the foul weather to find another lay-by, Frank Leonard took

CHAPTER NINE

Bev's mobile and started tapping out another number. Sophia shivered under the overhang of Micheli Tower. It was a different place in this weather, with wet reaching up at her from ferns as well as dripping down from trees and the old stonework. Even the ground beneath the sheltered spot turned out to be on a slight slope and running with mud. There was nowhere to sit, the smooth stone where she wrote her poetry was under the open sky and as wet as a low rock at high tide: no comfort anywhere here, and none in her head, either, as she stood and shivered under the overhang. What had she said to her mother?! Sophia couldn't believe she'd been so crude about Sol – but that wasn't the millionth part of it. Telling her mother she didn't love her, that had been the dirtiest, lowest thing she could ever have done. Every step of the way as she'd run the road her own evil had been jogged into her brain. The woman was a widow trying to cope without the person she'd loved. It hadn't been Sophia's way of coping and they'd fallen out about it big time – but to say what she had was unforgivable. More than anyone her mother needed her love because she'd lost Toni's, he wasn't there any more to deepen the sound of his sax round 'I've Got You Under My Skin', which he'd only ever played for her. Any hugs her mother would ever have in the months to come could only come from one person: her daughter, Sophia Micheli. And with her spiteful words Sophia had just taken away her arms. She wanted to bang her head against the old stone arch, to punish her body, to knock out of herself the thought of what she'd said: because there were rules in family rows – and she had broken the most important one of all, not to go over the line, not to move it from the particular row to an attack on the person. Her mother was right, she'd lost her boundaries. But most terrible of all to come to terms with, she had meant what she'd said. Try as she might she couldn't feel the love for her mother that she should.

Sophia pulled her drenched blazer round herself, shivered in the cold wet that had been clinging to her skin for an hour now. Just for something to do – other than stand and shake and taste the poison in herself – Sophia pulled out the loosened stone where she'd hidden her sheep's wool and some matches.

Both were dry. She found the baked-bean can, also dry, and peeled the paper label from it; then she looked around under the bushiest trees for dry kindling. If only she could warm herself in *some* way. But, no hope! The storm might be dying down a bit now, but it had come sideways across the marshes, and there was nothing in the copse that wasn't soaked. And as for baked beans, for comfort inside – she'd never brought the can opener she'd promised herself: everything here had stopped when Sol had surprised her. Without money London was out of the question for running off; but she couldn't even camp out here. And the realisation suddenly hit her: she *needed* her home right now if only for shelter – and therefore she needed her mother.

Sophia threw the beans into the trees, she churned the wool and the paper into the mud under her heel, and she leant against the old stone arch and started to sob her misery at the marsh.

Terry Ford was in the beach shelter on Sandgate front. The roar of the storm was down a decibel now but small shingle cracked at the lower panes and it was hard to hear the mobile.

'Royal George Hotel.'

'Yes. I'm looking for a room, a couple of rooms—'

'When would that be for, sir?'

'Tonight – through till Saturday.'

The sucking at the teeth could definitely be heard. 'I'm sorry, sir, we've got nothing. We're fully booked due to the—'

'Yeah, I know. The bloody flying weekend. You're the fifth place told me that.'

'It's always a busy time, sir.'

'Well, 'kin good for you!'

The trouble with a mobile phone is that you can't slam it down. All you can do is throttle the button – or hurl it away; so all the anger stays inside the caller, and right now the beach shelter echoed with Terry Ford's swearing till he started kicking the panels, and wouldn't stop till he'd smashed one to silicone crumbs.

Denise, the girl from the pub who was due to keep Donoghue sweet, stood watching him from the far end of the shelter. With each kick she winced and tried to get further back through the glass.

'Can't take him to your place!' Terry Ford snarled at her. 'If they're sitting on me they're sitting on your mum.' He looked out along the Sandgate road to where the camper van was still parked, just short of the Nelson. 'She's not what she seems, this snoop, she's one of a team. They'll know all about you! An' me, if I rub her out...'

'Who will?' Denise managed to ask. 'What team?'

'*Them!* The law. The filth. Whoever's watching! We've been sold down the river, girl, an' it's just good luck we haven't done nothing yet...'

The girl looked at him and shivered.

The mobile rang.

'Yeah?'

She listened and watched while Ford got control of himself and told of the hotel situation before he started taking further instructions from the man at the other end. 'Right!' he said, switching off. But he wasn't a happy man. He wasn't free of this business by a long chalk. 'Come on,' he commanded the girl – and they ran doubled over along the front away from the Nelson to where his own car was parked; which they got into and headed north into the marsh.

The back of the woman's camper van was misted up. It was like a police surveillance vehicle – like a gas or electricity or water board van that doesn't get a second look. People expect to see them about, with no idea that inside there might be four police officers 'sitting on' a suspect and ready to come charging out – or an electronic monitoring set-up with listening devices and cameras. This camper van had no curtains but windows of one-way glass, looking out where no one could look in, and inside it right now the woman was mouthing into a radio.

'No show,' she was telling someone. 'They should have been here by now, even in this weather. Either we've got it wrong or they're holed up somewhere else. Are you certain they made the snatch?' She listened to a crackly voice down the line and sighed. Surveillance was a cold, uncomfortable business with no toilet breaks. 'All right, I'll sit here,' she said, and wiped her breathing off the window to keep a good look-out on the Nelson.

With people forced by the storm to stay indoors at Marsh End, Lesley Micheli had to carry on as normal. In private, she could have thrown herself down and cried at what Sophia had shouted at her; but in her new business she had to go on with the show like a leading lady. Although there were the usual kettles and teabags in the bedrooms, she was making an effort to rise to the drama of the bad weather by offering hot drinks and biscuits in the dining room. But her unsmiling face and tight mouth dared anyone to sympathise with her about 'daughters' or 'storms in teacups'. And despite the sporadic gusting outside, when a ring suddenly came at the front door there was an immediate tea-room silence which would have been shattered by a dropped spoon.

Lesley went through and opened it, her uplifted

face saying she was ready for anything, a fight or an apology.

It was a man in motorbike leathers, his dripping helmet under his arm.

'Mrs Micheli?'

'Yes.'

'I'm Sol Barton. Jenny's brother...'

There was that inevitable moment before Lesley invited him in. 'Come through to the kitchen.'

'Thanks.'

Fortunes were being told in the tea leaves as the two of them passed through the dining room to the kitchen door which Lesley shut. Bird books reopened, ears cocked.

'Yes?' Lesley sat at the oak table and scraped back a chair for Sol.

Sol's hair was tied back in a rubber band, his eyes were calm and his smile was soft. He freed his steady hands from their gauntlets as he sat. 'I thought I'd better come and introduce myself.'

'Why?'

'Because I'm a friend of Sophia's. And I don't want to be a secret friend.'

Lesley's narrowed eyes told him not to soft-soap her.

'Why I've come is – Jenny reckons I sounded like the sex fiend of Romney Marsh the way Mum went

134

on. But I'm just a bloke, I go to work because I got bored at school, I met Sophia at our place and I asked her out. Boy asks girl to disco.' He put his crash helmet on the floor where it rocked on the slabs. 'I'm nineteen and I'm on the level. I'm not the local Romeo and I'm not a dirty old man – and if you don't want Sophia to go to the disco then we don't go.' He got up, scooping up his crash helmet. 'I thought I'd come and say that.'

Lesley's hand sat him down again. She looked him in the eyes, and he looked back, and smiled.

'I'm just me,' he said.

Lesley traced a knot line in the oak with a fingernail. 'I'm definitely not happy about the motorbike,' she said.

'Nor's Mum, but...OK, Mrs Micheli, that's all I came for.' He got up and bowed, creaking in his leathers. 'In *Northanger Abbey* this visit would have been a calling card.'

'You saw the telly?' Lesley's eyes went close to shining. 'I helped on the design for that production.'

'No, I read the book.'

She got up too. Sol looked towards the door, suddenly the awkward boy. 'Can I have a quick word with...'

'Sophia isn't here. I'm afraid we had a row—'

'Not over me?'

'No, over me, as it turned out. And she ran off.' Lesley all but started to cry.

'Where?'

Lesley shrugged. 'Just, *off*. Out of that door. She's not in the barn.'

'How long ago was that?'

Lesley looked at the kitchen clock. 'Too long, now.'

Sol's gauntlets came on, he went for the door to the dining room. 'I'll find her,' he said.

'She could be...anywhere!'

'She could be. But she won't. I know where she'll be.' And Sol went out to his Honda and kick-started the engine.

Sophia heard it above the sound of her sobbing as it came to where the road met the field edge out beyond the copse. Already she could tell the sound of its engine from any other motorbike's, and she knew that final little twist Sol gave the power before he turned it off. What was she going to do? He was coming here in the rain for some reason of his own – a damp practice under the overhang – and he'd find her in this pathetic state with her eyes cried out! Quick! She'd have to hide – and creep away when the chance came – because he wasn't going to find her looking and feeling the way she did. She turned to where the copse thickened, headed for the gap between two bushes, and slipped on the soaked leaves to go sprawling on the ground.

'Cav! Cav! You there?'

So he knew she was here; he knew where to find her. She pulled herself up, more wretched and muddy than she'd ever been in her life – her inside matching her outside. She couldn't face him right now! She had to get away! But in the slip and slither of getting up and getting pace, she went over again and knocked the wind out of herself.

'Oi!' he said, coming through into the grotto. 'What you playing at, Cav?' Before she could reply – not that she had any reply – he was pulling her to her feet.

She couldn't look up, the last thing she could do in the world was face him, let him see her awful eyes. She looked at the ground but she couldn't see it through the well of tears. She tried to turn her head away – but then his crash helmet and gauntlets were being thrown to the ground and with warm hands he held her cheeks and lifted her face up to his. He stared at her, and smiled, and kissed her.

'You've got mud on your face,' he said, after the first touch of lips. 'I love the urchin look.' And moving his arms to hold her, hug her, squeeze the wet out of her, he kissed her again.

And all at once this was so much easier than

speaking; words didn't come into it, there was no need for talk and explanation, somehow everything that needed saying could be said like this. Sophia kissed him back, and not with the playground peck she might have allowed Jonny Leete but with a sweet and long mingling of tongues that left her without the breath to speak. They broke off and looked at each other and kissed again, fiercer and finally.

'I guessed where you'd be,' he said.

'I'd like to be here for ever, like this.'

'No, it's too muddy.' Sol started leading her back through the copse towards the road.

But as she went, holding his hand and dodging the wet foliage, it suddenly struck her. Why had he had to guess where she was? She pulled hard and stopped him. 'Why did you come here anyway?' she asked.

'No secret to that, Cav. Your mum said you were out and hadn't got back.'

'You've been home, to Marsh End?'

'Sure. I went to introduce myself...'

'Did she tell you I'd gone too far with her and run off?' Sophia knew he had to know she was in a state over something, he'd asked no questions about her tears, and in a weird sort of way she suddenly felt ten years old again – with a big brother come to sort her out.

'Don't go thinking she asked me to look for you. I

wanted to. I wanted to know you were OK every bit as much as she does. I had a nightmare picture of you floating in a flooded dyke.'

'Instead it was me doing the flooding, blubbing like a baby...' She let him lead her on again, content to be ten for a bit longer. But she was back to sixteen when they got to the edge of the copse and he kissed her once more.

'Guess what I've got at the bike?'

'My mum – on the pillion.'

'No – lose ten points.' He took her to the Honda, and while the rain came on down he unstrapped from the pillion a crash helmet, matching his. 'It's new. For you. No one's ever worn it before.'

Sophia said nothing – she couldn't. She stood still as he lifted it over her head and put it on her, carefully strapped it under her chin.

'Seems to fit,' he said.

'Yup,' Sophia said. Which was all she could manage.

How old was the first girl you ever kissed hard
Not at the scuola, not in the yard
But out in the woods of Alássio
Deep and long and amoroso?
Was Lesley the hundredth – and did you care then
Whether you'd ever kiss her again?

Was it the first time you met on your own,
Backstage at the opera or walking her home
After the 'dress' or a starry first night
On some quiet piazza without too much light?
And did she kiss too or was it all you?
What did she say, what did she do?
Was she as joyful as God has made me?
Did she feel in that moment some deep jealousy
Of any other girl?

And how does she feel when she's not kissed
again?
How deep is her hurt, what hell is her pain?

CHAPTER TEN

St James' at Fallow Broad was a marshland 'redundant church': which meant that it didn't have a vicar and no one worshipped there because there wasn't the congregation around. But the door was always unlocked in the daytime for private visits, and the visitors' book and the offertory coin slot said that people did come to the Norman building. A leaflet of its history told of the time when the nave was used for secretly shearing sheep whose fine 'Canterbury wool' would be smuggled over to the Continent, and of when the tobacco brought back and hidden in the spire could be smelt two fields away. The church seemed almost proud of its colourful contraband past, and on the wall of the vestry was a framed extract from Rudyard Kipling's 'A Smuggler's Song'.

If you wake at midnight, and hear a horse's feet,
Don't go drawing back the blind, or looking in the
street.

Them that asks no questions isn't told a lie.
Watch the wall, my darling, while the Gentlemen
  go by!

Five and twenty ponies
Trotting through the dark –
Brandy for the Parson,
'Baccy for the Clerk;
Laces for a lady, letters for a spy.

And watch the wall, my darling, while the
  Gentlemen go by!

When Terry Ford and the girl arrived, the church had
a group of visitors every bit as hard and nasty as the
old Romney smuggling gangs. Bri Tingle was there in
the gloom with his two 'doormen' – the one who'd
driven the cars and the other, still stinking of sick,
who'd sat on Donoghue in the back. And Frenchie
himself was there being minded by the others –
hunched over in a pew and staring sullenly at the
ancient slabs.

'This is a right turnout!' Ford said, coming in.
'Who's she?' asked Tingle, looking at the girl.
'Denise,' said Denise. 'Who are you?'
Tingle ignored her. Donoghue looked up. He knew
Terry Ford, everyone knew everyone from the East End.

'So what's happening?' Tingle asked.

Ford walked over to the sprung prisoner and stood in the pew in front of him. 'Hello, Frenchie,' he said. 'Terry Ford. I'm looking after you.'

'Seen you on the telly. You're as crap an actor as you are a hard man.' Donoghue turned his look towards the girl. 'Only older, in real life.'

Ford folded his arms. 'I had it all nicely laid out for you, son. Good billet, tasty food, plenty to drink and a bit of skirt to remind you what life's like outside; to make your sacrifice worthwhile...'

'I've only sacrificed my prison cell,' Donoghue said. 'And my breakfast. Yet. Except from what I'm hearing it's all gone wrong...' Donoghue looked defiant.

'Oh, nothing crucial. A *detail's* gone wrong, but I'm still here to make life pleasant, so don't come on at me.' Terry Ford went over to Bri Tingle, lowered his voice. 'The main man's on his way. We hole up till he gets here, then do what he says. But I can't find a room nowhere, let alone two or three, the place is stuffed.'

'Got any food? We'll do in here till we get sorted. No one's coming praying this weather. An' if they do...' Tingle went over to the old oak door and bolted it – just as the ring handle turned and a knocking came on the other side.

The church froze; the knock had echoed round the old plaster like the crack of the Revenue Men. They had expected Terry Ford but Frank Leonard couldn't be here yet, not along from Brighton. With a quick word from Tingle the two minders took Donoghue – ran him – down the aisle towards the other end of the church and pushed him into the vestry, going in with him. Ford pointed to Denise, put his hands together as if in prayer; and she sat in a pew and bowed her head. He did the same himself in another part of the nave, kneeling – while Tingle went to the bolted door.

'We're shut,' he said to whoever was outside. 'Stocktaking.'

Ford raised his eyes to heaven.

'Well you c'n let me in all the same. I'm dripping out here like a de-fective shower.'

Tingle seemed to recognise the voice. 'That you?' he asked.

'It's not no one else.'

'The boat bloke?'

'That's it. Captain Bligh of the *Bounty*.'

Tingle opened the door a crack, ready with a fist if need be; but when he saw who it was he let the newcomer in. 'You're the *Pleasant Surprise*.'

It was Fred Kiff, who shook off his oilskin and shivered in the stony cold. 'Say one for me,' he told Terry Ford, who was getting up off his knees. 'Picked a bee-autiful day for it, didn't you?'

'What you doing here?' Tingle wanted to know.

'Who d'you think chose this place? I told the man, he told you. It's as good a den as any till he makes up his mind.' Fred Kiff seemed taller among the gang, a bit younger, and his voice wasn't so wind-blown in here, more hard oak than blown leaves. 'You brought the doings?' he asked Terry Ford.

'What doings?'

'The hair dye, what the man said.'

'It's in the car.'

'I'd get goin' on it, then, if I was you. You don' want it running down his face in this rain.' Kiff went to the door of the church and looked out. The weather had eased a bit, but the dykes were full and threatening to flood the fields and roads. He came back in. 'He can't afford to be long,' he said, 'there's a fog following this lot. We could be here till Hallowe'en.'

'Oh, no!' said Denise. 'Ghoulies! Don't fancy that!'

Bri Tingle looked at her, and winked. 'You'll fancy what we fancy, doll,' he said. 'I always wanted to be holed up with a bird in a cage...'

But there was work to be done, and with Frenchie Donoghue held down in a pew, Denise and Terry Ford got working on his hair. The sleek black he'd shown off in prison was trimmed, shampooed in rain-water from a butt and dyed white blond. 'An keep touching it up,' Ford told the girl. At the finish Donoghue was given tinted glasses to wear, and offered a choice about his strong white teeth.

'Bit of a trademark, your pearlies, we're going to tone 'em down a bit...' Terry Ford unscrewed a tin of dental make-up for films. 'Or we'll knock a few out – you choose.'

Donoghue looked at the tin and nodded. Like a circus lion he had his mouth held open by Ford while Denise started on the painting.

But there was a sudden rap at the door – and everything stopped as Tingle ran to it. One word from outside and he creaked it open – and in came Frank Leonard. Donoghue went to stand up to his full height, but he was pushed back down again. Tingle's men stood to doormen's attention, East End funeral style with their hands clasped in front of them. From over at the entrance Leonard eyeballed his hostage and walked slowly towards him.

'Judas!' Leonard spat at Donoghue. 'You got my messages inside...?'

Donoghue couldn't speak, they'd stuffed tissues in his mouth now while the dental paint dried. But he shrugged, like *I don't know nothing.* Leonard just stood and nodded at the con, every nod a diamond to be found, a score to be settled.

'You're taking us to where you stashed the stuff – an' if I don't come back with what I want, you don't come back either. *Ever*, you got me?'

There was no need for further words between them – Leonard's meaning was quite clear. He turned away and Terry Ford took him down to the church chancel and spoke to him quietly about the lack of local accommodation, his hands showing their emptiness of ideas. Leonard listened, then called for Fred Kiff.

'You know the score?' he asked him.

'I do, sir.'

'What about your railway carriage? We've got to hold him somewhere till the plane flies, Saturday.'

Terry Ford started nodding. 'Gallows Gap! That's off the beaten track. You've had drugs and guns in there, why not people?'

Fred Kiff looked at him. 'Because people have never been on Mr Leonard's shopping list. I've *never* beached people at Gallows Gap.' At Gallows Gap he had an old railway carriage that had been converted into a chalet in the days when Londoners took cheap holidays down in Kent. 'Couldn't hide this lot, not three days. The neighbours is easy so long as I don't bring dis-credit next door.'

Ford frowned, didn't understand.

'Overnight's one thing,' Kiff went on, 'but there's a whole lane of us down there, everyone's at it, an' some of the rest ain't angels, they definitely like bein' left alone.' He tapped his nose. 'An' they like rewards! They've got a thing about illegal immigrants an' ref-ugees, an' that's what they'll think we're about. They'd soon sell us down the river – they'd shop their kiddies for cannabis, they would.'

Leonard looked all round the church, back at Terry Ford and then at Fred Kiff again. 'So, what do we do?' he asked.

At which Fred Kiff suddenly took off his old cap and started rubbing his wet head. 'Well, if you've tried everywhere else, I do know someone with a couple o' rooms. Bed an' Breakfast on the marsh, down the road a bit from you. For a day or so. The old Revenge House. Used the barn all the time 'fore it was sold. Woman and her daughter. But you'll have to play-act the tourists...'

'Possible,' said Frank Leonard.

'No word of me, though, I'm Mr Odd-job, keep me out of it. But I can lead you there, an' you can say you're cut off in the weather.'

'Right!' Frank Leonard suddenly turned on his heel and walked swiftly to the back of the church where the others were. He was on top again.

'Stand him up!' he commanded.

Donoghue was stood up, the two minders holding his arms. He stared into Leonard's face, his mouth still open. Denise looked away, at the wall.

'Don't wet yourself, I'm not going to hit you! I'm going to tell you something. You're goin' to a civvy guest house, handcuffed to the bed for a coupla days, an' you're gonna behave yourself and not arouse no suspicions. Because if you do, Donoghue, you're dead; an' in the killing – before you *welcome* your lights goin' out – you'll tell me everything I need to know.' Leonard hadn't blinked his cold eyes once. 'An' don't tempt me, son, 'cos that might be the easiest way for us – a bit of torture an' a topping an' a splash off the boat. So we're doin' you a favour, you understand?'

Donoghue nodded that he did.

'An' shut your bleedin' mouth!' he said. 'Your breath stinks of prison.'

Donoghue spat out cottonwool and did so.

'Has anyone searched him?' Leonard snapped.

Everyone looked at Bri Tingle. 'No, Frank, they done him over twice like always. At Wyck Hill gate an' in the bus.'

Leonard swore. 'For drugs, an' snout, they did. But what about a little map, in his lining or somewhere? Might save us the bother of taking him across…'

They pulled Donoghue out of the pew, stood him

in the aisle, and gave his body a thorough and painful search while Ford went through his clothes.

'Nothing!' said Tingle, going for a wash of his hands in the font.

'But I've got something,' said Terry Ford. 'In his shirt pocket. What's this, Frenchie, a pretty picture?'

While Donoghue shut his eyes in disbelief, Ford handed Frank Leonard a creased and cracked photograph. It was a topless girl on a beach, and Ford waited for the dirty laugh. But it didn't come. Frank Leonard's eyes had gone to lizard slits as he looked at the picture. What he was staring at was a photo of his wife Bev.

'I've changed my mind,' Frank Leonard said quietly, 'I am gonna hit you!' And he doubled Frenchie Donoghue with a punch to the stomach and toppled him with a kick in the back, violence that wouldn't show – unless they hosed him down in a French mortuary.

Sol was taking it slowly on the shiny road, with Sophia hugging him tight around the waist. The crash helmet fitted, and even with the cold and wet round her legs she felt strangely comfortable. Holding on to Sol was a very natural position to be in. If only they were going somewhere else and not back to Marsh End. But Lesley Micheli had to be faced, there was nowhere else a daughter *could* go right now – and besides, she'd never been a coward, none of the Michelis were cowards. She would go back in and try to make her peace, and just have to see where things went from there. What was different now – what made it easier – was having Sol to hold on to: it somehow changed the way she saw things. *It meant she could feel sorry again for her mother.*

But Sophia didn't have any facing out to do, because when they got there Lesley had her hands full with sudden new guests. A car was parked in front of Marsh End and the front door was open with the rain blowing in. A girl came out of the house, pulled a coat from the back seat and went back in, closing the door.

'New arrivals,' said Sol, as he lifted Sophia's helmet off her head.

'Yup.'

'I'll see you then, Cav.'

'Hope so. Yes you *will!*' She found him a special smile. 'I've got a mobile, have you got a number?'

'Yes.' But he was all leathered up, it would have taken an age to give it. 'I'll ring you later – has Jenny got your number?'

Sophia nodded. 'And Marsh End's in the book.'

In front of the house now he was all business,

strapping her helmet to the pillion. 'Good luck! I'll be thinking of you.'

'And you, Sol…'

'I've learnt a new piece. Well, nearly got it.' He straddled his motorbike and kick-started it.

'What's that?'

'*Angel Eyes*. Ella Fitzgerald.'

'And Frank Sinatra,' said Sophia. 'He sang it a lot.'

'You know it?'

'Dad played it. For Mum.'

'I'll play it for you, Cav, in our place, soon – on our own, when we've got the time.'

'That'll be good.'

But time wasn't what she had right then. A man came out to move the car round to the back of the house and Sophia caught a glimpse of her mother carrying towels across the hallway. She waved Sol off and ran into the house to catch her before she went up the stairs. She just wanted to see her face, to look into her eyes, to make some contact again.

'Mum!' she said.

'Christ!' said Lesley at the muddy, flushed, wet face. 'I know!' she added, 'don't blaspheme!' Holding the towels off her she kissed Sophia on the dirty cheek, eyes wide open. 'Get cleaned up, I'm going to do a meal tonight…'

'Specially for?' Sophia waved a hand around to signify these new people, whoever they were.

'Couple in the Renoir, two men in the Degas and a single in the Turner. They asked for something to eat, they've been caught up in all this, came down for the fishing and had their boat battered in the storm. It'll cheer up the others too.'

'I'll help.'

''Course you will.' She held Sophia with a steady eye for that crucial second longer than was necessary. 'Chop chop, then!' And she hurried off up the stairs to put the towels in the en-suites.

Sophia went through to the kitchen to use the back stairs to her bedroom; she could get through to their own bathroom from her side. But she hadn't been in her room three minutes – standing looking in the mirror at what Sol had called an urchin – and thank God hadn't taken anything off, when in came a man, not even a knock.

'Easy! Sorry, babe.'

Sophia faced him, too surprised to be angry.

'Come up a floor too far. I'm under you...'

'Oh. Turner...'

'No, er, Smith. Mr Smith.' He was a man with big hands, a shaved head which shone, and a boxer's nose. But the simpering smile on his small mouth was what Sophia noticed most.

'The *room's* Turner. All the rooms have got names. After artists.'

'That's handy 'cos I'm an artist, a piss artist.' The man laughed. He was in a clean white shirt and black suit trousers, looked to Sophia like a musician backstage, brass, without his bow-tie and jacket. 'Anything you want, babe, knock on the floor.' And he went, closing the door as softly as a butler.

Sophia locked it, got out of her wet things and put on her dressing gown. They'd had the bird-loving creeps, she thought, now they'd got what Jenny called the FFFs – the fat fishing fraternity. And she wondered how much her mother would love running her new business now the rough end of the market was starting to use her place.

But whatever, she decided, she was going to make a show of giving support – to make up in actions for the diabolical thing she'd said.

CHAPTER ELEVEN

Frank Leonard didn't like to be crossed, especially by those close to him. But he always had his revenge and part of the pleasure he got from that came from choosing his own moments. One cocky young villain had waited a year with nothing but respect from Leonard before being taken for a one-way fishing trip on the *Pleasant Surprise*. So Bev could wait, he wasn't dealing with her just yet – but Gerald Scott and the weather were also crossing him and they demanded immediate action. Right now Leonard was in a foul mood at his planned meeting with the pilot at the Ashford hypermarket. They stood in Halfords looking at car radios.

'What you mean, it's off! What's off about it?' Leonard wanted to know.

'Everything's off, sir. Le Touquet's cancelled, their runway's under water, and Lydd has shut down all flights till the weather clears – thick mists rolling up now. I've been on to the air traffic controller – our beano's gone down the Swanee till next spring. Sadly.'

'Hang on – bloody *sadly!* You've still got wings…'

Scott nervously fingered a small car TV. 'But it's at Lydd and I can't get out. They've shut Heathrow, you know.'

'Yeah, I know. Today. They've shut the Transport Minister's mouth, *today*. But we're talking the weekend – or next week.' He took the TV out of Scott's hands before the alarm went off. 'Listen, Biggles – our man's tucked away now so a couple of days won't hurt. Saturday's not crucial no more so we just fix a new date.'

'That's another thing.' Gerald Scott took a precautionary step away from Leonard to look at a car compass. 'Your man's been all over the news. Any light planes going over to France, day or night, this weekend or next week are going to show up on the radar like stains on a nun.' He put his hand in an inside pocket, took out an envelope. 'I'm afraid I'm out, sir. There's your money back, Mr Leonard, every note of it.'

Leonard spun on his heel to look the other way. 'Put it away, you tosser! There's more cameras in here than Ronnie Kray's funeral. You're out when I say you're out!'

Gerald Scott sighed, looked to be putting the

envelope away but suddenly dropped it to the floor and kicked it under a display. 'No, I'm out, full stop.' And he walked from the shop, leaving Leonard to look around a bit longer before he bent to tie his shoes and retrieve his money.

'Full stop is right!' he said to himself. 'Don't forget, Birdman, I know where you live!'

The first real chance that Sophia and her mother had to talk was when Lesley drove her to the Digital South disco at Hythe Town Hall. The weather had calmed but a sense of storm hung about like guilt after a big row. With the barometer rising after the wind had dropped, the autumn marsh mists were billowing in off the sea and the car ventilation was working hard to keep the windscreen clear; the concentration needed to drive scooping the top of Lesley's attention. All the same, the sitting close and the being alone made private talk inevitable. And Sophia had waited for it so long that it was a relief when it started.

'You didn't mean what you said to me, did you?'

Sophia came in quickly. 'No. 'Course not. I was just angry.'

'It was very hurtful.'

'I s'pose you mean it to be when you're angry...'

Lesley's fierce sigh was lost in the blow of the fan.

'Well, it did hurt. If we hadn't been so busy I'd have lost sleep over it.'

'Me, too. I mean, I did. And I'm sorry. But they're definitely a weird lot to take in, aren't they?'

Marsh End had had an uncomfortable feel about it for thirty-six hours and it hadn't all been over the Sol quarrel. The fishing people definitely weren't the same as bird-watchers: perhaps, Sophia reckoned, because one lot loved and the other lot killed. They ruled the house in a way the other guests didn't, up and down the stairs wanting this, wanting that, in and out of the kitchen. Only the couple Sophia had glimpsed in the Renoir – a man with weird blonde hair and a girl – stayed in their room and out of everything.

'I've hardly slept a wink,' Lesley went on, 'I'm sorry we had space for them.'

'You said you hadn't lost sleep…'

'I meant not over you.'

Sophia rubbed her window and looked out at the dripping hedgerows. 'They're a sort of…London lot, aren't they?' For a moment she relaxed; she thought that what was going to be said about the upset with her mother *had* been said. For a moment.

'Don't you ever say anything like that to me again – even if you mean it.'

Sophia bent her head in submission, but perked.

Now she'd been ticked off officially – it was done and done with. *And* she was on her way to the disco where Sol would be waiting for her. 'Ignorance is bliss?' she asked her mother – and straight off cursed her flippancy. Why the hell did she say that?

'Some sort of pretence can help.' Lesley was squeaking her leather duster at the screen again, a busy hand to go with the deep, still statement which was to come. 'Nothing makes up for missing a man's kiss: but a kiss on the cheek can help.'

She hadn't stowed her leather before Sophia had leant over, kissed her on the cheek and given her a quick arm round the shoulder. 'That's not pretend, that's real!' she said. She understood what her mother meant; but wondered at the same time how she could use the same word for that peck and Toni kissing her – the way she and Sol had kissed at Micheli Tower.

And by the end of the evening, when her mother met her at twelve, Sophia was puzzling over the verb to embrace as well.

As she went in through the door – Jenny waiting for her, Sol discreetly inside – as she heard the DJ booming, saw the swirling lights and heard the thump of the music, she suddenly realised that this was her first time out since that terrible night at Club Seventeen. The night her dad had died she had gone into a place like this, excited, up for it, one of the gang with Eli – and she had gone home to death and mourning, deep grief and loneliness. Now she was dressed up again, out for the evening, and while there was no chance lightning would strike twice, she marked the moment as she went in through the door.

'Hi!' said Jenny.

'You don't mind?' Sophia murmured to the sky.

'Don't mind what?'

'Sorry, Jen – talking to myself.'

'Well, *he* won't mind. Lovelorn boy, inside. You look cracking!'

'Thanks. So do you.'

'So come on, why waste talent out here?'

They went in and up the stairs to the ballroom, where Sol was talking to a group of people; youngish but older than him; workmates and their partners, Sophia guessed. And was it her, or did he stand out of the crowd with his long shining hair, turquoise shirt and lively talk, making them laugh? One of the girls was giving him the eye, hanging on to his words so hard she was almost clutching at his shoulders and dangling weak knee'd against him. Sophia felt a sudden rush inside her: a squeeze of adrenalin like being called out in Assembly, a surge of excitement and jealousy which choked in her throat and hardened at her breast – and she couldn't believe how poised she felt on the outside as she walked over to Sol.

'Hiya, Cav.' Sol kissed her on the cheek, put a hand on her shoulder and introduced her to his friends. 'Sophia Micheli,' he said; and she had never heard her name sound so special.

The clingy girl drew off, winked at Sol as if to say, *I'll be around* and went to dance with one of the others. The group split, and Jenny was a real friend as she found a couple of people she knew and went to the bar for a Spring Boost, leaving Sophia with Sol.

He didn't talk a lot but he danced like a jazz musician – off the beat but knowing where it was, not scared to improvise but always in control, taking Sophia with him or following her lead according to the music, and where others stomped and sweated, he stepped and glowed. They didn't touch, it was facing, but where most people were dancing *to* each other instead of *with,* Sol and Sophia were a threesome: there were the two of them and there was the music. And he never once looked away from her. OK, eyes to the ceiling or focused at the floor, but never a shot over her shoulder or a look around that wasn't for the dance, wasn't for her.

This certainly wasn't Club Seventeen: clubbing, it wasn't. The Italian Association club was dedicated to the young stuff – the latest music and a school kid audience – while this was a company disco where a Managing Director did the twist and others let out of the office did slow grinds to just about everything; Digital South's annual party where no one would want to face anyone else tomorrow. But it was ideal for Sophia. There were raffles and a quiz, an annual award for performance (haw haw haw) and even an interval when the buffet was uncovered; all of which meant that there was plenty of opportunity for Jenny and Sophia, Sol and his mates to be a big party with running gags, catchphrases, embarrassing stories and drinks bought from a kitty: a *banda amicos*. So Sophia wasn't ignoring Jenny – who'd caught the eye of a tall young supervisor and was asking him in her direct way about the length of his legs. A great evening all round, Sophia thought, friendly and fun, and she'd have no need for a red face, or wiped-off make-up, or a skirt needing to be pulled lower for her mother's sake when she came back at twelve o'clock. That was, until about ten to midnight, when the DJ played the last segment of music. The lights lowered, eyes were closed, and the good-night smooch began to *Kiss Me in the Rain* by Barbara Streisand.

Jenny and her supervisor paired off, the Managing Director led his wife on, and Sol turned away from a hand offered by Clingy Girl to put an arm round Sophia and escort her deep into the middle of the floor where they could be hidden.

'So, how are you, Cav?' he asked, as they began a close shuffle.

'I'm all right.'

'Your mum let you come, then?'

'Apparently.'

They danced some more.

'Good song,' he said, at the Streisand.

'Did you choose it?'

'No, but it fits.'

There was another long pause while they moved slowly and Sophia decided not to say it. Then she did. 'Like us,' she said.

'What?'

'We fit.' And they did, looking round. The Managing Director couldn't get closer to his wife than their two big stomachs allowed, and Jenny and her supervisor were having to take it in turns to look up or look down to speak. But Sophia and Sol were comfortable, her head nestling on his shoulder and their bodies touching down to their knees. Neither of them spoke, it was perfect like that. The music stopped for a moment between songs; some took the chance to thank their partners and go, others came on to dance; but Sol and Sophia stood still, breathed deep and waited for the slow shuffle to begin again with *I Will Always Love You*. Sol relaxed his arm round her to hold her again a little closer; Sophia pulled herself a fraction tighter into him; and, pressing at each other, they somehow moved their feet to make small movements on the floor.

And, a growing new experience for Sophia, she could feel him against her in a way that she probably shouldn't. There was no undue pushing or thrusting at her but he was there, down there, a sort of fact of the dancing. She didn't move her face, she kept her arm round him, her hand on the back of his neck, stayed where she was; but inside her head she was shouting the questions at herself: what would her father say? What should a good girl do at a moment like this? And the answer was clear. Sophia Micheli had to back off, pull away – but she didn't want to; it was nice, natural, comfortable. His head and hers had lifted in pleasure as if they were listening to a beautiful phrase of music, and Sophia didn't want it to end. But it had to! She had to pull away!

She didn't, though, because she didn't have to. As the moment grew, it was Sol who pulled away, and with a wry smile, a touch of embarrassment, he said, 'I'm sorry about that.'

To which Sophia should have replied, 'OK' or 'Never mind,' or some such and gone on dancing further apart. But she didn't. Rash as ever she told him, 'Don't be. But come on, let's get a drink.' And she led him, at his own pace, towards the bar.

It was with Lesley hovering over in the doorway that Sol quietly asked her if she'd meet him the next afternoon at their place.

'Yes, please,' she said.

'Three o'clock?'

'I'll be there.'

'I'll play you *Angel Eyes*, I'm ready for you to listen.'

'I'm ready, too.' And somehow using her feet instead of wings Sophia crossed to say goodnight to Jenny and went out to her mother to be driven home.

It's God's design,
Divine invention
That gave the pleasure
To the valentine.

He set no sin
In His dimension
For pleasing one another
At our origin.

Don't lament
Meant emotion.
What He created
Has His assent.

It seemed Friday night innocent, a quiet drink in the Mermaid but Fred Kiff wouldn't normally have been in there at all; it was a tourist inn with the low beams of smuggling past. Smugglers present kept a thousand miles from these haunts, but when Frank Leonard wanted a word, a word was had – anywhere he chose.

'I've got the man an' he's got the map in his head. He's tucked up nice with your people, an' whatever Kent police is playing at, watching the Nelson, the rest of them are chasing our stolen cars from Harwich to Holyhead. Give it a day or so an' they'll jack it in and move on to something else...'

Fred Kiff sniffed into his brandy, kicked at the log fire with his toecap. 'Don't see the problem, then.'

'Bloody Biggles!' Leonard exploded. 'He's the problem! He won't take him! He's blown out of it on account of the poxy weather!'

'What about the ferry?' the old man asked. 'Hide him in a pack of day trippers?'

Leonard didn't bother answering that but snapped his fingers at the barman for another tonic. 'An' Tingle's car's no good – he can bring the stuff back later but he can't take Frenchie over while he's fresh, they'll soon spot a great bozo like him, specially if he *wants* spotting. Bri's for later.'

The drink came, double quick. Fred Kiff looked at

Leonard with a look that asked, *Why was he here?* 'Well, I can't fly – an' I'm not one of your strat-e-gists.' He showed his hands to the flames.

'An' I ain't wasting your time, Kiff. Remember that! You're in this for a packet!'

'So?'

'So it's gotta be the boat.' Leonard's voice had dropped to no more than a crackling twig in the fireplace.

Fred Kiff sniffed again, rubbed his old head. 'Storm's passing but there's a fair swell on an' a sea mist you could eat...'

'Exactly. So they won't expect nothing out, not for a night or two, they won't see you when you go. Then you come back empty an' they can have every plank up if they like...'

The old eyes twinkled a bit. 'Be extra, then,' he said. 'A fair bit extra...'

'Christ, there'll be enough for extra! You call it...'

Now there was the downing of the brandy glass and Leonard snapping up another for him.

'My ol' *Pleasant Surprise*, she's a sound old tub, sturdy as a lifeboat, I reckon we can make it if we go by night...'

'That's what I wanted to hear, Fred. You bring it out of Rye Harbour an' come in off Gallows Gap. We hole up in the railway carriage for a couple of hours an' go out on the tide. Tomorrow night.'

'As you like—' Fred Kiff thought for a moment. 'Tide suits OK, tennish. But I'll want—'

'You won't *want*, Fred, you'll *get!* Don't even say it. Them diamonds is going to make rich men of the lot of us. You can lay up your boat an' forget running the guns an' the drugs an' the booze for good...'

Fred Kiff leant forward and spat into the fire. 'Don't know about that,' he said. 'Wouldn't know what to do with myself wi' no skullduggery! Why kiss goodbye to the most sat-isfyin' employment on the south coast?'

CHAPTER TWELVE

It was 'go home' day at Marsh End. The bird-watchers were not enjoying the company of the fishermen, who filled the dining room with smoke and loud talk. When one of the women complained about hearing the F-word at breakfast she was asked if she'd ever heard it in bed. While the toast went cold, bags were packed and cars wiped free of leaves and twigs in the chilly mist and brought round to the front. As the insulted woman confided to Lesley, 'Sorry, dear, but they're not our sort.'

Lesley didn't know what to do. She took Sophia down into the cellar where no one could hear their voices or walk in on them. It wasn't a full-height cellar, except in one place at the far end where there was a square of decking over some sort of drainage sump into the dyke, so it was crouch or bend for stand and talk.

'They don't say what to do in the booklet,' Lesley said. The British Tourist Council assumed good behaviour; and from the fishermen's rough ways there'd be the world's end of a row if she asked them to go.

'What did they put on their registration forms?' Sophia asked. 'How many nights are they staying?'

'They left it blank, said they didn't know. A couple of days.'

'Where do they come from?'

Lesley shrugged. 'That's blank, too.'

'So they didn't fill the form in at all?' Sophia snorted. '*Can* they write?'

'They signed it, the one under you in the Turner did: said he'd do the rest later when his hands were dry.'

'Well, what about their car number? Couldn't we call the police and find out their address?'

'He's already said it's a hire car.'

Sophia crouched for comfort. 'Sounds fishy, Ma!'

'Well, they are fishermen!'

But the pair of them couldn't laugh. It wasn't crack-up funny and they weren't in the mood; their faces told how scared they were. With the last of the bird-watchers gone, Lesley and Sophia were alone in Marsh End with a gang of male roughs and one of their women.

Coming up from the cellar Lesley started cooking again. They'd demanded something to eat around six or half past so they wouldn't have to go out. They said their car battery was down, and there was no chance of Lesley saying no. Sophia helped with the table, then kept out of their way – Blondie and the girl were still in their room – and she could stay in hers while the others gambled at cards in the dining room. Their meal would be after Sophia was due to see Sol at three. She'd already chosen what she was going to wear – a black T-shirt, three-quarter trousers, wedge shoes and a quilted top over all; well, it was October. She was in the house yet out of it. Her body was there and part of her mind was too – nagging at her mother's worries over the rough guests. But her deeper thoughts kept coming back to the poem she'd written as she went over and over the night before, and as she thought about the secret meeting to come. She decided it had to be secret. She couldn't really leave her mother on her own with these people, not for long, but she'd tell her she was taking a crucial textbook to Jenny and she'd be quick. Mother Mary, why did everything have to be so *complicated* all the time? She faced herself in the mirror and tried to see what Sol would see. *Angel Eyes*? *Worried* angel eyes... Life was so unfair! No, she wouldn't be too long with Sol, but she had to meet him for a bit, she had to hear his music and make some soft music of her own with him.

With her clothes ready on the bed and her diary locked after writing, Sophia switched on her portable television, wanted to be heard doing something and not just mooning. Football Focus became news time, the main item all about the weather – the flood alerts, two people killed by fallen trees, the destructive seas washing away a field of caravans near Sheerness and now the thick coastal fog. There was a bit of police stuff – alerts at ports for someone on the run, the usual mix – then came the local news: Newsroom South East. That led with the storms, too, but in more detail, more Kent stuff; and the big local drama apart from the caravans was a missing girl from Sandgate. Someone hadn't been home overnight and her weeping mother feared she'd been washed out to sea in the storm. The thick weather prevented a proper search but they were very hopeful, blah, blah, blah… A picture was put up but it was a rave photo, all wide eyes and tonsils, no one Sophia knew.

Lesley called up the stairs; never one for letting others lie idle. She wanted the vacated rooms vacuumed and the bins emptied, nursing a thin hope of other people coming into the house. Sophia went through the communicating door from the old *Revenge* part of the house to the Victorian building. It was the Manet and the Monet that needed servicing; she had to take the rubbish bags and the dirty towels down and bring the clean stuff up. She threw the dirties out on to the landing floor and was closing one of the doors when she suddenly smelt the smoke of a no-name cigarette. The door of the Renoir had opened and someone was coming out.

It was the girl who shared with Blondie, someone she'd hardly looked at. 'He's in la-la land,' she said. 'Got any vodka and Red Bull, love?'

Sophia shook her head. They didn't keep any drink in the house except white wine and Cassis for Lesley's *kirs*. But her head froze even as she shook it. She was looking at the missing person, the girl from the television news – who wasn't drowned at all, but sleepy and sleazy at Marsh End! Sophia couldn't help but say it. 'Did you know your mum's looking for you – she thinks you're swept out to sea. She's been on the box...'

The girl swore, called her mother a filthy name. 'You got a mobile?' she asked in a quiet croak. Sophia nodded. 'Get us it, then. While Romeo gives me a break...'

'OK.'

The sound of a loud, dirty laugh came from the card school downstairs.

'Just you an' me!' the girl warned with a cautious look over the banister. 'Quick! Skedaddle!'

Sophia hurried through to her room. She didn't

know what the girl was up to, why she was locked up with Blondie, but she did know that the mother's weeping hadn't been a TV set-up. If the girl was on a secret weekend it still wouldn't hurt to let the woman know she was all right; or at least that she wasn't dead.

After all, Sophia would do it herself for Lesley when she went off one day with Sol...

She brought the mobile through to the main building and took the girl into the Manet room. 'Leave it in here when you've done,' she said. 'I'll be up in a bit.' She carried on with her duties. She emptied the plastic bags into the council bin at the rear of the house and carried fresh bags and towels upstairs, using her own *Revenge* way so as not to pass the card players in the dining room every time. In the kitchen her mother was busy at the sink, washing the local cabbage and carrots that Sophia had cut. And Sophia didn't know why, but as she went through she said nothing about the TV news and the girl – or perhaps she did know why, perhaps she didn't want to put another frown on Lesley's face.

When she got back upstairs the girl had finished her call but she hung on to the mobile; perhaps she hadn't got through. Sophia went into the Manet room and changed the towels. As she came out the girl met her on the landing again, carrying the rubbish bag from her own room.

'He's got a hell of a runny nose,' she said. And true enough, the bag was stuffed with crumpled tissues. 'I'll bugger the sewage if I put this down the pan.'

Sophia took the bag, held it at arm's length, looked at the girl's face. She hadn't slept a lot, that was for sure, she looked like Lesley Micheli in the weeks after Toni's death. If this was a secret weekend with a man she loved, it didn't seem very romantic: she should be *glowing*. Sophia would be, with Sol...

She went downstairs, the back way again, through to the foggy yard to throw the bag into the big bin; but as she lifted it something caught her eye. It was an empty box, the sort shampoo comes in, and through the plastic she could read the words: Just for Men – Scandinavian Blond. Blondie's hair dye! Well, she knew his hair wasn't for real, the quickest look had told her that – but this said it wasn't for real *recently*. He'd only just gone blond. So was that to please the girl – or was there some other reason? Sophia had emptied bins from the bird-watchers' rooms but they'd never had such secrets in them.

And there was something else, now her attention was caught. Tipping out the bag – rather than throwing it in tied up – she saw a batch of Marks and Spencer's labels and cut-off plastic tags, stuff from new clothes. *A man on a washed out fishing weekend who bought new gear?* And Sophia thought how carefully she'd chosen her clothes for Sol today, and how rough that girl looked. Had he bought them for *her?* There was definitely something very wrong about all this. Sophia hurried back indoors to say something to her mother; she couldn't leave her out of this now, she had to be told what she'd found - and about the girl. Mother Mary, she could be some sort of a hostage, or a slave!

But as she got inside the kitchen she heard a car on the road, slowing, stopping, and in trying to speak to her mother she had to follow her through to the hallway as the front doorbell rang.

It was two women, sisters by the look of them, about sixty, sixty-five.

'Hello, dear, we were just wondering if you had a vacancy. Just the two of us…'

'Well,' said Lesley. The house was suddenly quiet, the loud card game had stopped.

'We would have telephoned earlier or at least come here first—' one of them said.

'You *were* our first choice—' said the other.

'—but we were held up by a police roadblock, then this blessed fog came down.'

'Roadblock?' said a voice behind Sophia. It was the man from the Turner room who'd walked in on Sophia. Mr Smith. 'Did you say roadblock?'

'Only that we were held up, dear. On the A20. I'm telling your wife, you *were* our first choice, but—'

'But, but…' Bri Tingle imitated rudely. 'But we're shut.' And he turned Lesley by the shoulder to face him. 'You never changed the sign, did you?' He smiled grimly at the women. 'Sorry!' And he shut the door on them.

Lesley stayed facing him, her fists clenched, her eyes alight with anger. 'What the hell right have you to send business away? Who the hell do you think you are?'

Tingle bent closer. 'I'm Mr Smith, doll, I told you. An' you're the landlady, an' I've just bought your spare rooms. Don' worry, you'll get paid!'

'No, I'll get the police!' Lesley shouted, and she grabbed the door, yanked it open – with a hand at Sophia to drag her out, too.

'Behave yourself!' Tingle slammed the door shut with his foot. The two other men had followed him into the hallway. Tingle nodded at them and the phone wire was suddenly ripped from the skirting. 'We're payin' the piper, we're calling the tune. Now just you get on with your work an' both of yous'll be all right.'

'This is outrageous!' Lesley hit out at Tingle, and Sophia went for him hard – but it was only seconds before they were held tight, and struggling.

'Calm it! Calm it!' Tingle said. 'Don't have a baby!' He lowered his voice to what was meant to be reasonable. 'You're miles from sod all, we're in a right pea-souper, the phones are off an' the doors are locked. You're a couple of weak birds and we're three strong arms – let alone the ponce upstairs. So, do your women's work and you won't get hurt; be good an' we're out of here tonight. When we've had our meal and the light's going we're off, back to London. Then you can raise hell…'

Lesley was staring at him with hating eyes. Sophia was shaking in the grip of fear. This was like *Crimewatch*! For a horrifying moment she thought she was going to wet herself.

'An' when it's over and we've paid you, and you've give us half an hour to get away, you'll be well pleased, I tell you.'

'Drop dead!' said Lesley.

'Which is what you'll do if you play me up. Remember, doll, I know where to find you. Any time!'

And suddenly Sophia and Lesley were back at the death of Toni Micheli, clutching at each other, and shaking as one.

The dripping of the trees seemed to annoy Sol more than the pouring rain had done, catching his neck unawares. He stood at Micheli Tower, shivering in the damp with the clammy mist rising and thickening in the still after the storm. He looked around, sitting down in his leathers on a wet stone then standing up again. He pulled back his sleeve and looked at his watch, and fished in his pocket for his Hohner. He blew on his fingers, flexed them, ran the metal along his lips and started to play *Angel Eyes* as if he were an enchanter calling up a spirit. But no spirit came – he was there on his own with the sheep.

He gave it half an hour, then another quarter, and finally shoving the Hohner away like failed magic he picked his way back to the road and his motorbike. With a shrug he set off inland on the road from the marsh to Ashford; but at a near crossroads he suddenly swung round in an arc and headed back into the thicker mist on the way to Marsh End. Fifty metres short of the house he stopped, switched off his engine and idled into the verge. Parking up, he walked slowly and discreetly towards the lonely building. From behind a hedge he looked up at the windows of the first floor, to the room he knew was Sophia's. He checked his watch again – and in a sudden bold decision came out from the bushes and strode towards the front door of the house. Now his head was up and his expression was set, looking ready for a rebuff but about to take it on the chin.

Lesley had gone to the cellar for vegetables when

the front doorbell rang. Sophia was peeling potatoes, watched by one of the men who'd held her. But she was nearer to the hall door than he was, and she'd been waiting for something like this. At the first ping of the bell she suddenly threw the peeler down and flung herself at the door, pushing it open. But it was hard up against the burly back of the other guard, covering that exit. He swore – and Sophia opened her mouth to scream. But in the time it took to take breath enough, a hand from behind clamped her face and the other held her in a bone-breaking grip around the ribs.

The doorbell rang again.

'Anyone there?'

Sophia could hear the voice – Sol's – Sol Barton's, come to see where she'd got to! But at the sound of a man's voice and not two more old women, she was suddenly jerked off her feet and held there in the air, kicking and gagging with the vile hand round her mouth. Now neither guard moved, and nor could she, apart from her useless feet – all she could do was stare as the main man came out of the dining room and went to the front door. He opened it a crack.

'Yeah?' he said.

'Hi. I'm Sol Barton.'

'Sorry, mate, we're shut. Seen the sign?'

'No, I'm not after a room...'

Sophia squirmed, struggled, tried to bite the choking hand – but she was helpless against the strength of the man holding her.

'We're shut to everyone.'

'...I want to see Miss Micheli.'

I'm here! Sophia Micheli wanted to scream to Sol Barton – *I'm here!* Through the crack of the hall door she could actually see him.

'Sorry, pal, she ain't in.'

'She's gone out?'

'Well, if she ain't in, she's gone out. Come back Monday...'

Sophia saw Sol take a step back. He suddenly seemed so *sad,* so puzzled.

'Is Mrs Micheli in?'

'Look, I ain't got the time for all this,' the man at the door said. 'We're decorating...we got a job to get done...'

'Sorry,' said Sol. 'Only she didn't tell me that. Have they gone out together, Mrs and Miss Micheli?'

Sophia could see him trying to look inside, but the man moved to block his view.

'Must've done,' he said, ''cos they ain't here. All right?' He started to shut the door.

In despair Sophia saw Sol turn away, look along towards the rear of the house. 'But the car's still here. Did they go on their bikes?'

'Yeah, that's it, both of 'em. On their bikes.'

No we didn't! No we didn't! Sophia wanted to shout. *We're in here and we're prisoners!* But it all came out as dribble on the cold hand. *Don't go away, Sol! Be suspicious! Don't take that for an answer!* But Sol braced up, took a step further back, seemed about to say something else but didn't.

The man at the front door went on closing it. 'Gotta get on,' he said, 'keep the edge o' my paint alive.' And Sophia saw Sol finally turn away, looking like every jilted boyfriend ever.

And while the vile hand went on holding her hard, everyone inside stood like carved ice as Sol's footsteps crunched further and further away – followed by the sound of his Honda kick-starting, and a roar as it went.

Now Sophia was let go. She spat her disgust on to the hall flagging, wiped her mouth. But the main man was coming over to her.

'*"I wanna see Miss Mi-kelli!"* That your boyfriend, *Miss Mi-kelli*? he asked with a wide grin. 'Lucky 'im!' He leered at the others. 'But *has* he been lucky, we have to ask? Know what I mean?'

Yarf, yarf, yarf.

'Go on, you can say – your mum's not here.'

Sophia stared at him with the best she could of her dad's proud Italian eyes. She turned away, not going to give him the satisfaction of any sort of answer. But in reality this filth wasn't what was worrying her – it was Sol being so near to finding out what hell they were in, and then not! Plus the fact of him going off with the idea that she'd thought better of meeting him, thinking she'd cleared off out with her mum – so he wouldn't try again. Right now he was probably heading for Halfords to see what he could get second-hand on that new crash helmet.

But the men who were holding Sophia hostage weren't happy that someone had ignored the No Vacancies sign and called at Marsh End. With a word from the man in charge Sophia was yanked by the arm through the kitchen and pushed into the cellar, where Lesley was sorting her vegetables.

'You c'n come out in half an hour,' they were told, 'so long as Lucky don't come back!' And the door was shut and bolted on them.

'"Lucky"?' Lesley asked.

'Sol Barton. They gave him a stupid name. He came to the door just now. I was supposed to meet him today.'

'And what happened?' Lesley stared for some sign of hope.

'They fed him a story that we've gone out, they're decorating…'

'What did he do?'

'He bought it. He's gone.'

'*Shit!*' Lesley kicked over the sack of potatoes on the floor. 'On our own, miles from nowhere – no one else will come out here, not in this foul weather…'

Sophia started to pick up the spilled potatoes, righted the sack, a stupid routine action like a condemned prisoner tidying the death cell.

'What do you reckon they're about?' she asked her mother. 'Honestly.'

Lesley thought about it. 'I'm always honest,' she said at last.

'You don't know?'

'No, I don't know, Sofe.' Lesley put her arm round her daughter. 'They're obviously criminals of some sort, they've got that man upstairs the way they've got us – he's not one of them, I've heard them talking about him, they're taking him off somewhere tonight…'

'And where will that leave us?' But for all her wanting honesty from her mother, Sophia dreaded the answer she would get. '*Are* they going to clear off and leave us alone?'

Lesley looked at her and then at the ground. 'You missed one,' she said, pointing to a potato.

And without pushing for a further answer, Sophia bent to pick it up.

CHAPTER THIRTEEN

'I got your address from someone who drinks at the Nelson,' the woman from the camper van said. 'He told me your daughter works there.'

'But she's all right, haven't you heard? She's been found! Oh, God's so good!' Denise's mother was still in her mauve suit and cream blouse from the TV interview, her cried-out eyes and puffy nose making her look older than she was, like a sad nan at a wedding. 'You from the *Echo*?'

'That's right, Mrs...?'

'Clarke, with an "e". Mrs Clarke.'

'It must be a big relief, then, her being all right?' The woman's green eyes didn't blink as she smiled sympathetically.

'If she hadn't seen it on the telly she wouldn't have known I was so worried... I mean, she's a grown girl, she can live her own life, she's not signed in and signed out, I'm not her keeper...but when she wasn't at the Nelson I did think she'd been swept off

Sandgate beach, I really did.'

'Perhaps she's been swept off her feet? Suddenly? By a young man? Or is there someone you know about…?'

'No, she keeps herself to herself.' Mrs Clarke stopped, put a hand to her mouth. 'Here, you won't go printing none of this, will you? That's you said it, not me.'

'Absolutely, Mrs Clarke. Privileged information. So…did she say where she was right now?'

Mrs Clarke shook her head and dabbed at her nose with a tissue.

'How did she get in touch with you?' the woman wanted to know.

'On the telephone, o' course.'

'Of course, the telephone! Though it's not a stupid question – because it could have been by e-mail…'

Denise's mother found it funny. 'E-mail! Me! I've only just worked out how to get Channel Five! As for a micr-a-wave…!' She laughed on, her relief coming out now in mild hysteria.

'So, was it on her own mobile, or from a phone box, or – perhaps from someone's house?' The 'reporter' sounded very casual, her face not telling Mrs Clarke that this could be a crucial answer.

''Dunno about phone box or house – but she hasn't got a mobile. Nowhere to put it with what she wears…' She rubbed her nose, waggled it, making an unpleasant noise.

'Has anyone phoned you since? Or have you phoned out?'

'Not yet. Sorry. I will. Well, you people know she's OK now, and I'll let the telly know, they were very good. But there's no one else *to* know, to be honest.'

The woman outside now leant a little closer. 'Only, off the record, Mrs Clarke, we can find out where she is…'

'Can we?'

'Well, anyone can find the number she called from, dial 1471 – but with our…*newspaper resources*…the *Echo* can get the address for that number.'

'Really?' But Mrs Clarke suddenly clouded, relief gone, concern mounting. 'No, I don't want no one chasing her for no story… No offence, love, but she's got to live her own life.'

The other backed off. 'Absolutely. The laws of privacy must be upheld. We certainly try to do so at the *Echo*.' She became light and casual, making to go. 'But can you just give me *your* number so we can arrange a follow-up when Denise comes home? Get a nice picture of mother and daughter reunited?'

'Certainly, love.' And Mrs Clarke gave the woman her number.

'We'll be in touch, then.'

'Yes, lovely. And it's Clarke with an "e", as in Browne...'

'Bye.' The bogus reporter went, back to her van parked round the corner, where she sat at her electronic equipment and triggered her resources – to trace the number of the telephone used to call Mrs Clarke, find it was a mobile and be given its owner's registered address.

It was the eyes that got to Sophie. She had never been so aware how scary stares could be when they were held unblinking, on and on. Kids at her old school had stared her up, those boys on the Dymchurch bus still tried a defiant wink, the old bird-watcher men at Marsh End always gave her one over the tops of their guide books. But none of them went on, they were quick and private. Two of these men, though – these hostage takers, the assistants to the main man – they stared at her without pretending to be doing anything else; weren't scared of being seen eyeing her up. They almost took the clothes off her with their looks.

One of the men was chalk white, could have been an undertaker but for the tattoo and the earring; the other – with a hard, narrow face – wore a gold crescent on a neck chain and had to be of Turkish origin. The man with the earring seemed to be the one guarding Sophia, while his partner concentrated more on going where Lesley went. The Undertaker had small, rodent eyes and looked at Sophia as if he were crouching in some sort of lair, watching his prey. When she went to the bathroom, he went, too, and stood outside – she had to put a towel over the edge of the door, just in case, because he had eyes fit for the thinnest of cracks. It was disgusting, and it made Sophia feel dirty. And his expression never changed, it was just the pinprick little eyes – everything else going on inside his filthy head, with no doubts at all about what that was.

The other one – the Turkish man – looked at her differently. His face was thin but his eyes were big and brown, and with his staring went a smiling, and a rubbing of lips – and Sophia was made very aware of his tongue.

But it was the big man in charge who was the worst – because his eyes were so normal, and he could stare them without a blink longer than either of the others. It was this long, normal look, with him carefully not doing anything else of a leery nature, that seemed all the more sinister to Sophia – because as well as long, the look was always deep. He only had to turn his eyes on her to give her the terrible feeling that something creepy was going to happen; it was all so secretive and under the surface. She nearly jumped out of her skin when she was in the hallway carrying an extra chair through to the kitchen from the dining room. As she passed through she suddenly heard the rattle of an engine outside in the fog. She wanted to drop the chair and rush at the front door – but standing there in her line of vision was the big man, who just looked at her and stared. He didn't touch her or restrain her, he just looked long and deep – and she knew that she'd better not provoke him. He smiled at her, very normal, and said, 'There's a good girl, Miss Mi-kelli,' and as Sophia heard the vehicle going off into the distance, her heart froze – because there was no chance that anything would happen to get her out of this: away from this menace.

In Rye Harbour, Fred Kiff looked at his watch and interrupted himself from stocking up the *Pleasant Surprise*. He scurried up the gangplank, sat himself in the captain's chair, pulled out his mobile telephone and tapped in a number. It was quickly answered.

'That you?' he asked. Suddenly his face was no longer the old marsh handyman, nor even the skilful skipper, but more the hardened smuggler whose family had been fighting coastguards and Customs for two hundred years. 'Now, you listening? I got your instructions to give you...' He looked at the chronometer on his navigation panel. 'You make your move eight o'clock tonight, after it's dark,' he said, 'or twenty hundred hours, whichever comes the sooner.' He sniffed and smiled, took a rash bite at an old sandwich on his console. 'Now jus' listen, an' take note...' And with a change of tone – as if he were a computer helpline – he told the other end exactly what had to happen at eight o'clock. 'An' if you got any problems ring me,' he finished. 'But you ain't better not have!'

Bri Tingle clicked off his mobile and went out of his room. Sophia was coming down from hers, where she'd been getting some painkillers – the Undertaker close behind her. She had a headache, but what was hurting more inside was the sick feeling of knowing she should have thrown that chair at the main man down in the hall and made a dash for the door. All right, it was locked – and he'd have caught her and had to restrain her – but at least she would have been making an *attempt*. As it was, all that she and her mother were doing was these villains' bidding, and waiting, waiting, waiting.

Now she was coming down from her room and he was standing outside the door of the Turner room.

'That the call, just now?' the Undertaker asked him.

'Shut it, will you?! I tell anyone what they need to know when they need to know it. Right?'

The Undertaker kicked the skirting board.

Sophia looked at the boss. Right now there seemed to be a new urgent sort of threat in his voice, it was strained just that bit higher, thinner. Up to this moment he'd been roar and bluster; now he seemed on edge, tenser. But as he saw her coming to pass him along the landing, he changed, he went into that normal, *normal* look again. He stood aside with his back to the wall to allow her past, like a teacher in a school corridor.

This was a narrow corridor, though, and he knew it – and Sophia suddenly wasn't thinking straight. She had to pass him and she should have turned her back on him, but in a half step she was at him already, and passing the big man. And he was making himself bigger, not pressing himself back to the wall as much as he could, but just standing there. Then he relaxed his stomach, let it out as she passed him – with her eyes turned away looking where she was going, and she was forced to brush against him. She pulled herself in as much as she could, but he didn't make any concession, and she couldn't avoid the touch.

'Easy!' he said. 'Just room for two! Miss Mi-kelli.'

And she was past him, and trembling – while all he did was go back into his room, which he could have done in the first place. How dare he treat her like that? That's where Sol was so different – and how Sophia wished to hell that he hadn't accepted as gospel what this villain had said to him at the door.

Because despite her anger, more than ever now she was churning with what could be in store for her and for her mother.

Across the fog-clothed fields at Middle Marsh Manor, Frank Leonard's den in the basement was like an operations room. Spread across the full-size snooker table were maps of northern France on which several small airfields were highlighted in yellow marker – but he was having to ignore those now. Instead, he was tracing the route from St-Valery-en-Caux on the Normandy coast down the D20 towards Rouen. He swore as his nail ran down the thin line, his eyes following the map through a magnifying glass.

There was a knock at the den door. He didn't answer, didn't look round. There was another knock, more apologetic, then the door was gently opened.

'It's only me, Frank, it's Bevvy.'

Now he turned. 'Stop using that stupid name!' he said. 'You're not sixteen. What you want?'

'I only brought you some tea.'

He ignored that, went back to the map. Bev put the tea on a ledge, but she still hovered.

'Ain't you gone?' Leonard asked her.

'No, Frank.' She came towards him. She was attractively dressed and beautifully made up. She smelt discreetly of *Lingering Love*, Leonard's favourite perfume. 'I just want you to know…I'm always here for you,' she told him. 'Busy times like these, you always liked me helping you, I had a part to play – and I'm still here for that. I'm a bright girl.'

Leonard looked round at her with a look of hate on his face. He left her with it, went back to the map.

She took a step back. 'I don't know what's going on,' she said.

'You'll find out,' he told her. 'In due course. Everyone finds out what's going on with Frank Leonard – when he decides to take action…'

And with that, she had to go.

Sophia and Lesley were being kept under even closer observation by the gang. While Denise was still keeping Donoghue high and quiet in their room and Tingle was upstairs in his, in the old *Revenge* kitchen Sophia had to sit at the table while Lesley stood at the cooker – all the time their minders' eyes hard on them. But guarded by a man each, the necessary things had gone on. Right now, as the cooking came to a climax, Sophia kept her head down in a B and B brochure: her dad had taught her back in London how you don't make eye contact in tricky situations, you never provoke. And these were professional muscle, and had she or Lesley made a move towards the door there was no doubting what they'd do. As the cooking went on, the old oak in the room sweated a thin clam of tension like the *Revenge* going into battle formation.

Sophia turned the pages over and over without reading a word, too aware of the danger in the air, of the smell of gunpowder before the spark. Ready eyes were all about. Something was going to happen – because every sign told her the explosion was near.

But in all that, still she couldn't help but think of Sol Barton. Before coming here earlier he'd have gone to Micheli Tower and waited for her, and when she didn't show – and he'd also got the brush-off at the door – he'd have decided that she'd blown him out, probably on account of what had happened in the dance. He'd have put two and two together and reckoned she'd had second thoughts. It had been her *choice* not to go; he'd been out of order at the disco, letting his feelings show, and although she'd been polite about it at the time, she'd thought differently later.

And how could he know about the poem she'd written…?

Sophia sat and stared, but cooking for five big appetites was giving Lesley plenty to do. She had two pots of potatoes on the go, with the local vegetables from the cellar and two packs of Auntie Bessie's Yorkshire puddings from the freezer – and the meat was a smallish joint she was having to roast slowly so as not to shrink it too much.

Twice the big man had been down to find out how long things would be. Now he came a third time, and Lesley looked up sharply.

'Not you!' he said. He pointed at Sophia. 'You.'

'What do you want?' Lesley cut in. 'Ask me – you leave her out of your business!'

The man rubbed his hand over his shining head. His normal look had gone: now he was like a stretched balloon that needed bursting, or a wino who needed a drink. 'Don't get out o' your pram! I want to ask her a question.'

'I told you I can answer any questions!' Lesley came away from the cooker.

'Yeah, but you're busy with my dinner – which I want on bloody time. She can tell me what I want to know.' He looked across at Sophia. 'Chop chop, Miss Mi-kelli!' he said. "Fore I have to give your mum a slap.'

Scared out of her mind, but not wanting to think of her mother getting hit, Sophia shut the brochure and took herself over to the door, her mother's eyes skewering into the man as Sophia went past her and up the stairs.

'In here!' the man said at the Turner room.

'What?' Sophia asked. 'What do you want to know?'

He pushed her inside and shut the door behind

him. 'Up there,' he said, jerking his head at the ceiling. He deliberately dropped his voice. 'What's all that?'

Sophia looked up. 'Well,' she said, 'we call that a light – *a light* – and above it is a ceiling. *A ceil—*' She couldn't help herself, she had to pretend she wasn't scared.

The man's hand swept back; but he stopped short and swore. 'Don't you get funny with me!'

Adrenalin surged into Sophia's system. She took a quick breath, all her body would allow her. 'Oh, you mean the stars? Stars, that's what they're meant to be,' she told him, edging for the door.

But he put himself in front of her, his eyes half shut and his pupils big. 'I thought they was just spots, in patterns, for when the light goes out, in the dark...' His voice was low and secret, like a kid at a party who's steaming up to try something on.

'Exactly. It's the sky at night. The northern hemisphere. Just a bit of fun...' God, Sophia thought, what a stupid choice of words!

'An' I do like a bit of fun.' But he was folding his arms like an executioner, not looking fun at all. 'Come to think of it...' he pointed to the ceiling '...there's the sky up there, an' who's the other side of it up above, in heaven?'

Her dad, Sophia thought, having to see this bullying going on.

'*You*. For me down here you're in heaven up there, up above the stars – in't that right, Miss Mi-kelli?'

Sophia stared at his face, which was going a deep red. He was coming to something. 'That makes me dead,' she said, in someone else's voice.

'I tell you what it makes you, sweetheart, it makes you what you are, a little angel! An angel who can take me to heaven! Know what I mean?' He wet his lips, slowly.

Sophia wouldn't look at him: her mind had frozen with what he'd said. The waiting was over.

'What's *am-or-oso*?' he was going on.

She didn't answer; she was eyeing the door, the window, the heavy ashtray by the bed.

'What's it mean? *Amoroso*?'

Sophia knew all right, but she wasn't dirtying the word by saying it to this filth. As she watched him, though, he went for the bedside table and opened the drawer.

'You a good little kisser, are you?' And from it he took Sophia's diary, the lock split open and the leather torn like an assault. '"*Deep an' long an' amoroso*"!' he read out, his voice thick in his throat. 'Very sexy! I fancy some o' that, an' a bit more besides...!'

'You bastard!' Sophia screamed. She ran at him, grabbing, kicking. He'd violated her, breaking into her private writing. 'That's mine, that's private! That's to my dad, not for your ugly eyes!' She screamed again, jumping for her diary which he held high above his head, laughing. 'Give that back!'

'Reach up an' get it!' he sneered. 'Come on, let's have you!' And to Sophia's horror he started going to his trousers with his free hand.

She was on her own with him. She could shout the house down and no one would hear her on the deserted marsh. She would fight till she died but still this big man in control of the house would do what he pleased – his wanting eyes told her that. And now he took a step towards her.

As the bedroom door suddenly burst in on them and in rushed Lesley, screaming loud. She threw herself at the man, her face filled with hate and her kitchen knife raised to stab him. Fast behind her clattered the others, but already she stood, prepared to kill, between the big man and Sophia. '*Stop it!*' she shouted. 'Get out! Leave her alone!'

The man just laughed. 'I'll have you put down the cellar again if you carry on like that!' He tossed the diary on to the bed. Rocking on the balls of his feet he eyed up the quick way to disarm her without getting a cut.

'*Leave her! You'll deal with me!*' Lesley screamed. She pushed Sophia further behind her, backed half a pace herself, took the others in – and suddenly reversed the knife, to hold it pointing at her own throat. 'One move this way – any of you – and I'm ending it!' She was out of breath, could hardly get this said. Both hands took a fierce grip on the knife's handle. 'If it doesn't matter...whether...I'm...here or not, I'm gonna get my *death* on your charge sheet!'

Sophia shouted. '*Mum! No!*' What was she doing? Nothing was worth that!

'I'll be in the reckoning when they catch up with you!' Lesley was on her toes ready for the thrust; and Sophia knew she meant everything she said, glaring with wild eyes at the big man. Her body froze as her mother's real threat held him there for a moment.

'Leave it, Mr Smith,' the Undertaker said. 'It's mucky enough...'

'Yeah,' his partner agreed. 'We've got our hands full wi' matey an' the other girl. You c'n have all the fun you want, the other side.'

There was a long beat before the man took a step back. But his eyes were on Sophia all the time with the glazed look of unfinished business. And suddenly he dived in and ripped the knife from Lesley's hands.

'Don' think I give a toss whether you come out o' this or not!' He swung to his men. 'Now take the ol' woman downstairs while I finish what I started!'

CHAPTER FOURTEEN

The camper van – the vehicle Sophia had heard – had driven on past Marsh End but at the next bend it had pulled on to a dyke bridge that was used by the farmer to get to his field.

The woman got out of the van – and had the sort of shock she'd once given to Sophia. Down at her feet, coming up out of the shroud, was a young long-haired man in leathers. She just had time to get back inside and lock the door before he came to the window.

'Who are you?' she asked through the glass.

'Never mind. Who are you?'

'You tell me who you are and I'll tell you who I am. You're clearly not hedging and ditching.'

Sol Barton made a winding gesture at the window so as not to have to shout. The woman opened it a crack.

'I'm a friend of a girl in that house, and I'm looking out for her. So who are you?'

'Denise Clarke?' The woman asked. 'In the Bed and Breakfast?'

Sol shook his head. 'Sophia Micheli. She lives there – and her mother owns it.'

The woman opened the van door very slowly as if it ran on glass bearings.

'There's something going on in there!' Sol said. But as he said it, he saw into the van with its electronic equipment. 'What's all this? What are you doing here? Who are you, MI5, police?'

'No, love.' A soft answer with a harder voice. 'Neither of them, but official, you might say... On the right side.'

'On the right side of what?'

'Never mind. But nothing for you to worry about.'

'I'm sorry but there is! There's a man in that house who says he's decorating – when the place has just been done up. And he said my girl and her mother both went off on bikes – when Sophia's mum hasn't got a bike. That's why I doubled back, why I'm watching...'

'Well, now you can leave the watching to me—' The woman sounded like an unconvincing social worker. She reached behind her and took out a pair of imaging binoculars, came out of the van and focused them on Marsh End.

'Hang on! It's my girl who's in there!' Sol pulled at

the glasses. 'How long does it take to knife someone, or shoot, or...rape them? You might be watching, but you won't be *stopping* anything!'

The woman backed off and laughed. 'Oh, come on – don't be so dramatic! I tell you it's all under control. Trust me.'

'You're Customs! *Are you Customs?*' Sol suddenly clicked his fingers. 'And they're drug running.' He turned a full circle and came back to her. 'Well, let 'em go! Shout at them! Let 'em know we're here! Or call the police and go in and get them! Anything! Scramble a helicopter, call the riot squad, whatever it takes! I tell you, they've got my girl prisoner—'

The woman shook her head. 'Your girl's fine till we do something just about as stupid as any of that! *Then* they'll use her as a bargaining chip – *then* she's in danger, can't you see? When something happens, when any of them come out, we act. But going in now would only blow the whole operation.'

Sol suddenly blew himself. 'No! I've had this! We're on different agendas, you and me! You want *them*, I want my girl. *She's* what's important, not your bloody *operation*! I'll call the police!'

'Is ten million pounds important?' the woman asked him. 'Could you use a good percentage of a big reward?' She turned away for a quick look towards the house again, but when she turned back, Sol had gone. And half a minute later she heard the kick-start of a motorbike and a soft throttle as he went off up the road and into the swirl.

Lesley screamed and struggled against the two minders taking her downstairs from the bedroom, Tingle with one hand round Sophia's throat – when the first rev of the bike was suddenly heard. For a moment it sounded as if it was coming towards the house, but then there was nothing more – whoever it was seemed to have gone away. Lesley screamed again – but as Tingle turned his attention back to Sophia there was another sudden roar from outside, and a shout.

'Let 'em out! The police are coming!'

It was Sol! In the shock Sophia suddenly threw herself free and ran to the window to tear the nets aside. Could she yell to him outside? This was life and death now! But Tingle was straight at her.

'You lot!' Sol shouted at the house. 'Let those people go!' For a second Sophia saw hope again with Sol on his Honda revving and shouting outside. 'Be the worse for you if you don't!' he yelled.

'Hold her!' Tingle shouted. In a flash the Undertaker pinioned Sophia, his dirty hand clamping her mouth again. Grabbing up his mobile Tingle ran out to the landing and banged in a number.

Below them Sol still prowled his bike round and round, its beam showing up the thickness of the fog, his voice cutting through it with hoarse shouts. 'You're on a loser! The law's on its way! Let those people out!'

But gripped there by this filthy man, Sophia knew this wasn't the end of the ordeal. Sol was playing for time outside but time was what they didn't have in here. What these men were up to was big and serious. Urgent. It would take a second to stab her; a *split* second to shoot her. And when she and her mother had been taken care of, Sol would be an easy target down there on the other side of his headlights.

Any strength Sophia had left drained from her. Sol being there had boosted her, but he should have waited for the police. Out of love he'd tried to save her – but he'd made his move too soon.

In his kitchen at Middle Marsh Manor, Frank Leonard was studying a chart of the Channel that Fred Kiff had brought in. They were routing to St-Valery-en-Caux when Kiff's mobile suddenly rang. The old man listened, and swore. 'They've been fingered!' he told Leonard. 'Law's on its way to Marsh End. Tingle wants to know what to do.'

Leonard didn't have to think about it. 'Get out!' he said. 'Tell 'em to get out! They got time?'

Kiff asked and Tingle reckoned no, not without blowing it: there was someone at the front and the police not far off. Kiff looked at Leonard, and Leonard stared at Kiff. 'Then tell 'em the other way out!' he said.

Kiff pushed the mute on his phone and shook his head. 'I do that an' there's people'll know I'm in on this! They know I used the place for stuff when it was empty; they'll soon put two an' two together if Tingle gets out through my way in... Ten million pounds' worth of diamond heist is a bit different to a couple of kilos of baccy.'

Leonard grabbed Kiff by the shoulder, shook him. 'You tell 'em!' he said. 'A – because we ain't gonna get found out; an' B – because if you don't, they'll soon put two an' two together all right – of you! Into your box, for the funeral!'

'All right, Frank, all right!' And reluctantly Kiff started giving Tingle instructions, Frank Leonard shouting 'Cock up!' as he went for the door.

He pushed the listening Bev aside, doubled up the staircase to his bedroom and started throwing clothes into a sports bag as Bev followed and stood watching him.

'What you doing, Frank?' she asked.

He didn't reply.

'Frankie? What you doing? Where you going?' She

came into the room and over to the four poster where he was folding a shirt on the bed. 'You never said you was going with them, not tonight.'

'Well, I am.'

She pouted, put a hand on his back, ran it down his silk shirt. 'What about me? I'll be on my own. You never used to go on trips 'ness you took me...'

He shrugged off her hand. 'Well I do now.' But his voice was even – too even and controlled.

'When you coming back?'

He lifted the bag. 'In a minute.' He took it down the stairs and out to the car on the gravel. Fred Kiff had gone already and had left the gates open. Leonard threw the sports bag into the boot and went back upstairs with a cat's tread.

Bev was at his wardrobe, choosing a tie from the rack. 'Take this,' she said, 'you always feel good in this.'

'I feel good anyway.' But his eyes were cold. And on the bed she suddenly saw a topless photograph of herself.

'Where d'you get that?' Her poise suddenly left her.

'Guess where! Off Donoghue. He's had little Bevvy Leonard for company all this time...'

Bev backed off. 'Not from me,' she said, 'I dunno where he got that, I never gave it to him.'

'No?'

'He made a play for me while you was inside, but

I turned him down, I turned everyone down...'

'Yeah?'

'I never looked at another man, Frank, honest. It was Donoghue looked at me. I was a model, people do look...'

But in Leonard's looking right now his eyes had taken on the glint of pleasure he always had when he went out on a punishment job.

'I was always loyal to you, Frankie, I loved you, I *love* you – an' I've never ever let anyone come near me. I swear it, on the life of my mum and dad...'

'I'm gonna say goodbye.' Leonard said. 'And when I've said goodbye, *slut*, you're gonna think twice before you even say good morning to any other man, even the hospital doctor...'

And while Bev backed away from him, Leonard calmly turned to the bedroom door and kicked it shut from the inside.

'Send 'em out or we're coming in!' Outside Marsh End Sol was throttling and shouting, revving round and round – this side of the house, that side – and shouting at the building from front and back as if he were a squad of people, not one.

'Two minutes! We're giving you two minutes!'

Tingle was in the kitchen now with a knife at

Donoghue's throat, instructing his men. 'Put them women in there!' He pointed at the pantry.

Grabbed roughly, their feet not touching the ground, Sophia and Lesley were pushed into the tight dark space and the door locked on them.

'An' as for you!' Tingle grabbed at Donoghue's hair and twisted his head back. 'One little move off you an' it'll be a whelk wi' no cockles who comes to France!' And he dropped his hand to make his meaning clear.

But before he could make the man wince there was suddenly the sound of sirens – and through the window the foggy reflection of flashing blue.

'They're coming!'

Outside, Sol shouted to the woman from the camper van who'd come running after him. 'Right! This is when they'll do their worst in there!' He revved the Honda to a new pitch. 'We're coming in!' he yelled.

'Foller me!' shouted Tingle in the kitchen. 'You next an' you at the back!' The Turkish bouncer pulled Denise, and the Undertaker did as he was told and went last, pushing Donoghue with a handgun as Tingle grabbed a flash lamp and ran to the cellar door – to go clattering down the stone steps, the others following.

With a last roar outside, Sol opened the throttle and balanced himself.

'What's the point of being brave now?' the surveillance woman shouted, trying to pull him from his machine. 'They could kill you!'

But Sol shrugged her off. With a loud shout he put down his head and raced his bike top speed at the kitchen door.

'*Caaaaaav!*'

Crack! With a great splintering of old wood the door split aside and Sol and the bike smashed through – brakes thrown on hard as the wet machine slid on the stone floor, sparking and crashing into the stove and sending a pan of gravy spinning into the air. Spanner in hand Sol leapt up, his eyes all round ready for fight. But the room was empty, just a banging and screeching coming from the pantry door. He ripped it open – to see Sophia and her mother huddled inside, terrified, shaking. Sophia threw herself into his clutching arms, sobbing and moaning and hanging her weight on him.

'Cav!' he said, and as she shook in his arms he bent to her and kissed her, long and hard and deep, there in front of her mother. Sophia held tight on to him and kissed him back, the wet of the mist on him – and her tears and their mouths mingling in the relieving melt of the moment. They took a breath for words, but it was Lesley who spoke.

'Please hug me, too!' she said in a quiet, shaking voice.

And the three of them stood and hugged each other till their arms ached.

'Gawd help us!' Tingle was on hands and knees, peering along the damp and dripping passage stretching ahead. Following his instructions he'd led the gang to the deep sluice at the far end of the cellar and with help had lifted the heavy metal of the sluice cover. Below him a shaft a man deep dropped into a low, earthy passage. On its roof a cordless light was fixed. He pushed up at it and it lit, showing a line of old oak spars like pit props and another light at the further end. He crawled ahead and the others followed, strips of matting along the floor making things easy on the knees. Tingle switched on the other light.

'Someone's done this up all right!' said the Undertaker, his voice coming cold and flat along the line.

'It's like a grave,' Denise said. 'I'm claustrophobic!' But they reached the end of a thirty metre stretch where another shaft led up to a trapdoor. Tingle pushed at it and climbed into the Marsh End barn; and silently, with a hand clamped hard over

Donoghue's mouth, the rest followed and scuttled to its far end where there was a small door, just as Kiff had described it.

Tingle put his head cautiously outside, but they were far enough away from the house not to be in the view of any eyes trained on Marsh End. A narrow track led out into a copse where the trees gave cover, and with bent runs – both Tingle's men on either side of Donoghue now – the party scuttled across the road away from the house and slid quickly down the dyke bank.

To be met by Fred Kiff with his small boat, well out of sight.

Nothing was said. Tingle and the others crammed themselves into the low craft while Kiff pushed off against the swollen run of the water and took them silently round three bends to where his car sat, doors open ready.

'Smart!' said the Undertaker. 'Them ol' smugglers knew what they was about.'

'No more'n us modern boys,' said Fred Kiff. 'At least, you've gotta hope so, 'cos I'm your ticket now.' And with the car weighed down to the wheel rims and Donoghue held hard in the back, the old man took them the long way round to the final rendezvous at Gallows Gap.

CHAPTER FIFTEEN

The police threw a net round the area but the gang had gone. In the Marsh End dining room Lesley and Sophia were being counselled by a woman police constable while the camper van woman and Sol stared dislike at each other across the table. Mother and daughter were holding hands, Sophia squeezing Lesley's till the bones cracked – devastated at what her mother had threatened to do, and certainly would have done; been ready to kill herself to save her daughter from assault. And filled with self-disgust, Sophia thought of the secrets that man had read in her diary, her dislike for a mother who'd then shown such courage, such sacrificial love.

The policeman in charge was plain-clothed, with the careful accent of promotion. He was youngish with a hard haircut a lifestyle apart from Sol's locks. He'd come from headquarters in Maidstone and clearly held the respect of all the police in the room – more of whom seemed to be arriving by the carload.

All over, there was an air of getting somewhere, but with no one knowing where. How the gang had disappeared so quickly was a mystery; but one thing was already certain – forensic had been up to the bedrooms and out to the bins, and using the internet via their laptops they knew that the fingerprints in the Renoir room were Patrick 'Frenchie' Donoghue's. They knew they were on the tail of the man who'd been sprung from the prison bus – and that he was blond-haired now instead of black.

Sophia noticed that the detective seemed to accept the woman Sol disliked as being some sort of expert, and not about birds.

'How would anyone have a convenient illness on cue outside a hospital in Totham?' he asked her. 'Right where his team's waiting?'

The woman shrugged. 'Heroin?' she suggested. 'There's plenty of that in prison. Dropped in his breakfast tea? If he's not a user it'd bring on something looking like a heart attack to a novice – and they could time it, prison transfers always leave on the dot.'

The detective inspector eyed her. 'Heroin put there by who? Whom? A bent warder?'

She stared back at him, then nodded slowly. 'Perhaps someone bending in more directions than one,' she said.

'...And organised by someone top level who wants those diamonds found.' This wasn't a question; the DI sounded certain.

'What?' Sophia was on her feet. '*What?* Is that what this was all about? Was I nearly *raped* on account of some organised scam? For some company's *diamonds*?'

The woman folded her arms. 'Conjecture,' she said evenly. 'It'd take some proving.'

But Sophia's sudden anger controlled the room now. Everything stopped as she jabbed at the detective inspector. 'You're after diamonds, are you? Well, *she's* after diamonds, she'll have some, thank you! Lesley Micheli!' Sophia pointed at her mother with a shaking arm. 'Only, she wants the legal sort, the sort you stick in your window or paint on your sign, for running a legal business, by sweating your own sweat. *Decent* diamonds – not got by assault and fear and *rape*!'

'You weren't actually—' the woman began.

'You shut your mouth!' Now Sol was on his feet.

But the woman wouldn't be quietened: 'For the record it was ten million pounds' worth of industrial diamonds, stolen from a cutting room in Antwerp. Would you want someone to do a quiet prison sentence and come out to that as a pension?'

'I don't understand,' Lesley said quietly. 'Will someone explain what this woman's on about?' Her voice was shocked, fatigued, a victim's voice. And by its timidity it had to be addressed.

'The Antwerp diamond job was the biggest there'd ever been, all over the news at the time,' the DI said to Lesley quietly. 'You may remember it – a major heist for which we only got to prosecute one man for violence. And, normal practice, when the diamonds weren't recovered after a certain time, the insurance company had to pay out for the loss.' He looked at the bird-watcher woman. 'But at any time the goods are found, the insurers get their money back...'

Sol hadn't moved far from the woman. Now he went right up to her, face to close face. 'So you're not MI5 or Customs, are you?' he asked her, a deep loathing in his voice. 'You're *insurance*. It's you wanting your pay-out back! You risked these people here for your balance sheet. You planned this – you fooled those villains into thinking they were doing it, but you're as deep in this jailbreak shit as they are!'

'*Are they here?*' Sophia was at her, too. 'Are these poxy diamonds somewhere here in the house? Are those people coming back when you've all gone away? Have we got to sleep in wet beds where we've pee'd ourselves with fright listening for a bang on the door?'

'Now, love...' said the WPC.

'Come on, *where are they?*' Sophia shouted. 'You

owe it to us to know!' She pointed at Lesley. 'She...was ready to *kill* herself!'

The woman looked at the DI. 'France,' she said reluctantly. 'Donoghue hid them in France five years ago.'

'So they *won't* come back here?'

'Not if we catch them they won't! First things first.' The DI broke off to take a report from a detective constable coming in. 'All local flights are grounded,' he told the room. 'We can call off the airport unit.' He paced about and came to Sol, the man with the real local knowledge. 'So where d'you reckon a *boat* would go from, off this shoreline?'

Sol shook his head. 'Dunno. This is all smugglers' coast, has been for four hundred years. Harbour's too dodgy, but they'll get off from some flat beach on the next tide. Could be anywhere from Sandgate round to the other side of Camber...'

Sophia sat down again with her mother, let the business go forward around her, still in shock staring her disgust at the insurance woman.

'Choppers are grounded with the rest...' the DI was saying. He shook his head and sighed. 'If we start a search of all the beaches right now we'll be looking till dawn...'

'By which time they'll be well away,' the insurance woman said, 'high tide's at ten o'clock...'

'We *could* get lucky – and pigs might fly!' The DI started giving instructions to his DC to at least kick things off: but the looks all round the room were gloomy, like people on a search for a missing person who they strongly suspect is already dead. Maps and charts were spread on the tables – but they hadn't got the creases flattened when there was a knock on the door and in from the foggy kitchen came a PC with a woman. A battered woman.

'Someone we found wandering on the road, guv.'

Everyone had turned to look. The woman being brought in was unsteady and clutching her stomach, and her face was a pulp of bruise and blood.

'Mother Mary!' Lesley said.

'Beverley Leonard,' the PC told the DI, 'she was on the road outside her manor house…'

'You're *Frank* Leonard's wife,' the DI said. He went to her and sat her down, clicked his fingers for a glass of water to be brought. 'Has Leonard done this to you?'

The injured woman said nothing.

'Why's he done it?' the DI asked.

'Who said he had?' Bev Leonard looked defiance at the room but she accepted a tissue and blotted some blood.. 'I could have fell off a wall…'

Now the DI was crouching at her. 'If you did, you fell the right side, Bev. You fell this side, our side, the legal side.' He stared at her while she sniffed. 'You must have had enough...'

The WPC started to dab at Bev with antiseptic from a first-aid kit but she didn't wince. The room was silent. The DI seemed to know that he didn't need to prompt too hard with questions. He let the first aid go on, then he quietly said, 'Only, Frank Leonard will know you've been here with us. Helping us with our enquiries...'

'I'm bloody not!' Bev tried to shout at him, but it hurt too much and she started to whimper. 'I'm no grass...'

'He's not to know that, is he? When the heat's off and you're out of hospital, he'll likely come back and finish the job he started...'

'Only if you say I was here. Picked up and *brought* here!' Bev hissed.

'Needn't be me saying anything, Bev. There's a lot here looking at you...'

Bev Leonard looked round the room, at Sophia and Lesley, Sol and the camper van woman – but they all stared back, everyone prepared to meet her eye.

'If you're worried about any come-backs, I promise we'll keep your secret,' the DI said. 'Once we get Leonard inside you could sell up what's legally yours of Middle Marsh Manor and go somewhere no one knows about. Start again. New identity. New life.

We can fix that for you.' He smiled at her gently. 'How d'you fancy Spain? You must reckon you're worth more than this...'

Bev lifted her head, for a moment, tried to look proud through her injuries. Then suddenly, she broke down and cried. Her voice wailed in an animal cry of despair, a creature in a trap. 'Yeah, he's done this,' she finally said in a low, trembling voice, her words hard to follow coming from her battered mouth. 'He's gone off me...and he's blaming me...for something I haven't done.' She caught her breath on a sigh, and nodded. 'You're right, as it goes.' No one moved, hardly breathed. 'I think he will come back an' do the rest...' She raised her arm to her face and wept, and wept. 'So...what do you want to know?' she said at last.

Notebooks were out, but only in the mind; no one made any move which could have stopped the woman answering. 'Just say what's going on,' the DI said. 'Take your time.'

She did. She had to be finding it hard to betray her husband, but the pain on her face at any shift of her body told them why she had to do it. 'They've lifted Donoghue from prison an' they're going to get their diamonds. He's stashed them somewhere over near EuroDisney or somewhere...' A fresh glass of water was slid in front of her across the table. 'The plane's off so they're going in the boat...'

'We guessed that. Which boat, love?'

Bev tried to sip the water but it was too difficult now, her mouth was still swelling. 'Fred Kiff's – the *Pleasant Surprise*.'

'*Fred Kiff!*' Sophia straightened. 'We know him – they've stolen his boat?'

Through her pain Bev turned to Sophia with East End pity. 'Get real, girl! He's in it up to his dirty little eyes. He's the main man round here after Frank. You want soft drugs, hard drugs, guns? You want smokes and booze? He does odd jobs all over as cover an' he's into every nook an' cranny going.' Carefully, slowly, she looked round the room. It had to hurt to talk, but she went on. 'He had this place stuffed full of gear before you came and spoilt his game. He was still getting it out of your barn last month!'

'Christ!' Lesley suddenly banged a flat hand on the table. 'Dealers! Criminals! *Filth!* They're *everywhere!*'

'And more to the point is where some of them are right now,' the DI said – and he turned to Bev Leonard again. 'So where are they, love?'

Bev Leonard took stabs of staccato breaths. This was the crucial moment; she could still pull back from here. But after a stare at the DI, 'They're at Gallows Gap, in Kiff's old railway carriage,' she told him. 'He's dropped them off and he's taking his boat round from Rye...'

'Right!' said the DI – and he was about to give an order into his walkie-talkie when he caught himself mid breath, fell silent. He paced to the kitchen door and back, and suddenly stopped. 'We've got Interpol and the coastguards and Customs cutters. Now, if this man Kiff can get across the Channel...so can we, and we can track him...'

'And...?' asked Sol.

'We can please this lady,' the DI said, turning to the insurance woman, 'like it or not. We follow them to the goodies, let them get their sweaty hands on them, then we drop our net.'

'Just catch 'em!' Lesley shouted. 'For what they've done to us. Our bruises won't show like hers but they'll last a hell of a lot longer!'

The DI came to her. 'Mrs Micheli, Frank Leonard won't do more than three years for assaulting his wife – but he'll go down for twenty if he's caught with the biggest diamond heist ever...'

Lesley drew breath.

'...He'll be off the scene till he's an old man.'

And at last she nodded – while everyone else saw the sense in that. Quickly, the police operation was put into action. Sol and the WPC ferried cups of tea, but Lesley sat back at the table with her head in her hands. 'I thought coming here was a good idea,' she said, tears rolling again, 'for me, and my daughter. Away from the crooks and the filth of London...'

The WPC leant over and patted her hand.

'...But you never get away from them, do you? I was so wrong – villains are everywhere, town and country...'

The DI came off his radio. 'Are we all right in here?' he asked Lesley. 'Use it as our Incident Room – for now?'

Lesley nodded, waved a consenting arm at the room.

'You're definitely in the right place,' Sophia told him, looking at Bev Leonard who was tenderly lighting a shaky cigarette. 'Well named. You know this is the old Revenge House? I reckon she's given it back its name, sorting the man who did that to her...'

The battered woman just blew out smoke.

Lesley shivered, came to put her arm round Sophia, hugging her into her side. 'Maybe you were right, Sofe. You and me, perhaps we should be thinking about getting back to London...'

An icy skin seemed suddenly to wrap Sophia. 'What!'

'Well, I've had an offer of theatre work.'

'Not Bee du Pont?'

Lesley frowned. 'How did you know?'

'It was written on the pad,' Sophia said, but it was hard working her mouth, she was frozen by what her mother had just said.

'Well, nothing rash – but I'd like to think about taking up her offer, going back to where we came from – Tottenham, Eli, your Club Seventeen, the old life...'

Now the ice had gone. Sophia's face was hot, her neck red. This was the woman who would have died for her – but who still didn't understand. 'No! Let's stay, please!' She looked at Sol, back at Lesley. 'You can do it all from here! I want to stay now.'

'And I know why, Sofe, and I sympathise – but...'

'My life has changed.' Sophia grabbed her mother's hand. 'I love Sol,' she said.

Bev Leonard began to wail softly as she smoked, and the rest of the room went about its business.

Lesley took Sol's hand, too. 'Well, what are motorbikes for?' she asked. 'Toni and I managed – him in Rome and me in Leeds. You can gatecrash us in London any time you want!'

Sophia couldn't believe this. They were still two cats in a bag, nothing had changed.

Or had it? she wondered, as she, Sol and her mother stood there together. Weren't they different cats now? After what had happened to them both, couldn't there be more purring than clawing in the future...?